P9-CAO-687

FIGHT
for the
VALLEY

**Center Point
Large Print**

FIGHT for the VALLEY

WAYNE D. OVERHOLSER

CENTER POINT PUBLISHING
THORNDIKE, MAINE

This Center Point Large Print edition
is published in the year 2007 by arrangement with
Golden West Literary Agency.

Copyright © 1960 by Wayne D. Overholser.
Copyright © renewed 1988 by Wayne D. Overholser.

ISBN-10: 1-58547-982-9
ISBN-13: 978-1-58547-982-5

Library of Congress Cataloging-in-Publication Data

Overholser, Wayne D., 1906-
    Fight for the valley/ Wayne D. Overholser.--Center Point large print ed.
        p. cm.
    Previously published in 1960 under the pseudonym Lee Leighton.
    ISBN-13: 978-1-58547-982-5 (lib. bdg. : alk. paper)
    1. Large type books. I. Leighton, Lee, 1906- Fight for the valley. II. Title.

PS3529.V33F54 2007
813'.54--dc22

2006101767

Fight for the Valley

BOOK I   THE BOY

chapter 1

TOMMY GORDON GOT OFF THE TRAIN at Winnemucca in the cool, early part of the morning. For a time he stood at the edge of the loading platform looking around, the brittle sunshine almost blinding. He had never seen a town quite like this one with the sage-covered hills to the north and south, the maze of shipping pens on down the tracks, the twin lines of steel catching the sunlight and shining like silver ribbons that finally were brought together by distance and then were lost to sight against the horizon.

Bridge Street, Winnemucca's main street, was different too, he thought, as he turned north from the railroad and strode along the rickety sidewalk in long, springy steps. He breathed deeply of the sage-scented air, thinking this was just about the way he had thought a cowtown would look. Here were the tall false fronts, many of them weathered by sun and wind so that the letters painted across them were almost obliterated. Here were the hitch rails, the water troughs, the dusty street, the saloons with the swinging doors that were still now.

Tommy walked to the river and back along the other side of the street, noting the places where he might get a job. The town slowly came to life. Swampers were cleaning up the saloons, occasionally coming outside

7

to empty buckets of dirty water into the street. One of them straightened and put a hand to his back as he looked at Tommy. He said, "Howdy, bub," and went inside.

Business men appeared and opened up the stores and banks, calling greetings to each other. A young woman unlocked the door of a millinery shop and opening it, stood there a moment as she looked up and down the street. She smiled at Tommy as she said, "Good morning."

He paused and said, "Good morning," wanting to ask her if she had any work for him, then went on. He could do a number of things, but trimming hats wasn't one of them.

He passed a livery stable. A cowboy stood in the archway, smoking, apparently in no hurry to start for wherever he was going. He spoke to Tommy, looking at him curiously, the cigarette dangling from his lower lip. Tommy was surprised that he wasn't wearing a gun.

On impulse Tommy stopped. "Are there any ranches around here where I could get a job?"

The cowboy grinned. "You a bronc twister, buster?"

"No. But there ought to be chores to do around a ranch. If there are, I can do them."

The cowboy shrugged, flipped his half-smoked cigarette into the street, and turned away, saying, "I dunno where you'd start."

Tommy was disappointed, but he had no right to be. He'd be lucky finding work in town, and it was too much to expect to fall into a job on a ranch. He had breakfast in a café near the tracks, flapjacks because that was the cheapest, and when he paid, he asked, "Have you got any work I can do?"

The man behind the counter shook his head. "Hell no. I'm lucky to find work for myself."

"I'd work cheap," Tommy said. "Just for a place to sleep and my meals."

The man shook his head again. "That's all I get, and it ain't enough to divide."

Tommy laid his bundle on the counter. "Can I leave this?"

"Sure." The man tossed it behind the counter. "Get your dinner here if you've got money to pay for it."

"I've got money," Tommy said, and went out, wondering how long he would be able to say that.

He started at the upper end of Bridge Street and worked along one side of it and then the other, asking for work at every place he came to except the millinery shop—even the bank and the saloons. Usually the answer was a flat "no," sometimes a "maybe next month if business picks up," which was no help at all because he had about nine dollars in his pocket and he couldn't make it last a month.

Twice he passed a big, blond man with a star on his vest and a gun on his left hip, carried butt forward. Tommy had planned to lie about his age if anyone asked. He was sixteen, but he was big enough to be taken for eighteen, and he was strong enough to do the work that any average man could do.

He returned to the café at noon, tired and discouraged and afraid the blond man was going to start asking questions. The last time the law man had seen him he'd watched him curiously. A little too curiously, Tommy thought. The one thing he didn't want was to land up in a stinking jail.

"Any luck?" the man asked.

"No." Tommy drank the water the man placed before him, and shoved the glass back across the counter for a refill.

He ordered ham and beans, and when the plate came he asked, "You know of a ranch where I could get work?"

"No, I sure don't. Summer's the wrong time to hit town. This burg ain't ever on the boom except during shipping time when the big cowmen like Mike Dugan drive their herds in. The crews hang around for a few days blowing their money and getting into fights. If you was here then, you'd get a dozen jobs offered you. Now?" He spread his hands. "You won't find a damned thing."

Tommy paid for his meal and asked for his bundle. The man gave it to him, saying, "Leaving town?"

"Looks like it. Who's the big man with the star I saw on the street?"

"Town marshal. Name's Ben Lampe. You might go see him. If there's a job in the country, he'd know it."

"I figure I'd better keep away from him," Tommy said. "I don't want to see what his jail looks like."

"He won't jail you if you don't do nothing." The

man wiped a dribble of sweat off his chin. "We get a lot of tramps riding through who stop off for a meal or to steal something. Some of 'em ask for work. Not many. But you're young, kid. Be better if you went to see Ben. If you don't, he might start looking for you."

Tommy considered it a moment and decided the counter-jumper was right. He said, "Maybe I'd better."

He remembered seeing the jail, and went directly to it, not knowing whether he'd find Lampe there or in one of the saloons. But Lampe was in his office, sitting at his desk eating his lunch from a dinner pail, a jar of coffee beside the pail. He was finishing some kind of berry pie when Tommy came in. Lampe wiped a sleeve across his mouth, leaving a dark stain on one cheek.

"Come on in, son," Lampe said, holding out his hand. "I'm the town marshal, Ben Lampe. I seen you on the street this morning, and I heard you were asking for work."

Tommy shook hands, instinctively liking him. He often felt that way about people when he first met them, especially if they were the kind who made an impression on him. Some were like milktoast and he didn't care one way or the other, but this Ben Lampe was a man you didn't overlook.

"I'm Tommy Gordon." His eyes met the marshal's blue ones. "I didn't have any luck."

"Didn't figure you would." Lampe motioned for him to sit down. "When a boy jumps off a freight and starts asking for work, he don't have much of a show."

"I didn't jump off a freight," Tommy said. "I rode a passenger train into town. The early one. I got in before the town woke up."

"That so?" Lampe leaned back in his swivel chair and rolled a smoke. "Suppose you tell me about yourself. Ran away from home, didn't you?"

Tommy didn't say anything for a moment. Lampe thought he was lying. Natural enough to think that. The question now in Tommy's mind was whether to lie or tell the truth. He had a hunch that Lampe would know if he was lying, and if he did, Lampe wouldn't have any use for him. He'd better tell the whole story.

"I don't have a home," he said. "My folks died four years ago when I was 12. Burned to death in our house on a farm in Missouri. My Aunt Sadie Gordon came and got me. She sold the farm and took all the money that was in the bank. She never gave me any. She runs a boarding house for railroad men in a town called Prairie City. It's in Nebraska. She never liked me and she didn't want me, but she was my only relative, so she had to take me. She worked the tail off me, Mr. Lampe. Part of the time I never got to go to school. I didn't even finish the eighth grade."

Tommy clenched his fists, his gaze on the marshal's face. He went on, "You don't know what it was like, Mr. Lampe, not getting to do anything and being treated like a poor relative while she kept all the money that my folks left. Finally I told her I was leaving. She said good riddance and gave me a few dollars and said to get on the next train. That's what I did and now I've got just a little over eight dollars. I've got to find something to do, Mr. Lampe."

"Why did you come to Winnemucca?" the marshal asked.

"My money was running out, so I knew I couldn't go much farther, but the main reason was I got to talking to a man on the train and he said Winnemucca was a good cowtown. I thought maybe I could get a job here."

"I can check on all this, you know," Lampe said.

So Lampe didn't believe him even when he told the truth. "Check and be damned," he burst out. "I didn't lie to you. All I want is a chance to work, even if it's just for my keep."

"Any kind of work?"

"Anything I can do."

"I didn't figure you were lying," Lampe said, "but I've got to check on your story if I'm going to help you. Not saying I can, mind, but then again, I might."

Tommy stared at the floor. He was tired and sick and discouraged. What would he do after his eight dollars was gone? He said, "I guess I ran away, all right, but Aunt Sadie didn't want me back. 'Keep going,' she said."

"I'll send her a wire." Lampe got up and scratched the back of his neck. "You tell a straight story, Tommy, and you looked me in the face when you told it, so I don't figure you're lying, but I've got to make sure."

13

"I guess so," Tommy said.

"I can't find you a job that'll pay you any money, but maybe I can get you a place to live. Come shipping time, you might catch on with one of the nabobs, though I don't really figure you can." He motioned toward a cot in one corner. "Might as well take a nap. It'll be awhile before I hear from your Aunt Sadie."

Tommy remained where he was for a few minutes, not having the slightest notion of taking a nap, but he'd sat up on the train all night. A moment later he woke with a start, his head bobbing against his chest. He got up, and walking to the cot, sprawled across it and fell asleep at once.

It was dusk when Lampe shook him awake. "I heard from your Aunt Sadie. She sure don't want you back. Come on, I might have something for you."

Tommy followed Lampe outside, groggy from sleep. He paused beside a trough long enough to douse his face with water, then caught up with Lampe. They strode along the nearly deserted street, Tommy almost tripping over some loose boards in the sidewalk. When they reached the millinery shop, Lampe opened the door and motioned for Tommy to go in.

"I can't trim hats," Tommy said. "This is the only place I didn't try this morning."

"And the only place where you had a chance," Lampe said. "The work isn't trimming hats. Fact is, you won't have much work to do. The main thing I'm interested in is finding a boy with gumption. I figure you've got it."

14

Tommy stood just inside the door, looking around at the hats on the counter and the table in the back of the room with ribbons and feathers and all the foofaraw that went with millinery work. The girl he had spoken to that morning came in from the back.

"Tommy, I want you to meet Dora Lind," Lampe said. "Dora, this is Tommy Gordon."

She extended her hand and he took it, liking her just as he had liked Ben Lampe when he'd shaken hands with him. "I saw you this morning, Tommy," she said. "You might have asked me for a job."

"I don't trim hats," he said.

She laughed. "I don't need you for that." She turned to Lampe. "Did you tell him?"

"No."

She looked at Tommy again, closely, and said, "You're sixteen, Ben told me."

"That's right."

"You're a good, clean-looking boy," she said. "I need one I can trust. Oh, there'll be a few chores to do. Dishes to wash when I'm busy and a little cleaning up to do, but what I want is someone to stay here at nights. Saturday nights especially."

"That's when I'm busy," Lampe explained. "We get a lot of cow hands in town every Saturday night and they kick the lid off. Then there's the bums who get off the trains. They're the ones I'm really worried about. You may have trouble, but nothing you can't handle. I'll see you have a gun."

"My cooking isn't bad, Tommy," Dora said.

15

She was young, about twenty, Tommy guessed. He could return her compliment, for to him she was a good, clean-looking girl, with hazel eyes and brown hair done up in long curls. She vaguely reminded him of the last school teacher he'd had in Missouri. Outside of that teacher, he'd never been around a young woman. Now the prospects of staying here with Dora Lind bothered him, although he didn't know why. But he couldn't turn it down.

He swallowed and looked at Lampe who was watching him closely. He said, "I'll take it. I don't know if I have any gumption or not, but I'll try to look out for her."

"Good," Lampe said. "Wouldn't look right for me to stay here, but I guess nobody'd talk about a boy your age living with Dora."

"You worry more about my reputation than I do," Dora said testily. "Come on back to the kitchen. This is the time to try my cooking, Tommy. Maybe you should have tried it before you said you'd stay."

Dora took Lampe's arm and they went through the door to her living quarters, Tommy following. The way Lampe looked at Dora, Tommy had a hunch he'd better not let anything happen to her, or the marshal would have his hide. Then he wondered why they weren't married. But it was their business. It was something he'd better not ask about.

chapter 2

IN MANY WAYS the weeks Tommy lived with Dora Lind were the most satisfying of his life. She fixed a cot for him on the screened-in porch. At night she locked her front door, and latched the back screen. Ben Lampe gave Tommy a shotgun which he leaned against the wall beside his head. Every night before he went to bed, he pulled his cot forward so that it was between the screen and the door. Anyone coming in would stumble across it.

Dora kept a small revolver under her pillow, although she admitted she'd be too scared to use it if she had occasion to. She said she slept better with Tommy on the back porch, although she realized someone might break in through the front door. But it was unlikely, she told him, because Ben Lampe or his night man made the rounds up and down Main Street every hour or so.

At first Tommy thought both Dora and Lampe were worrying about shadows, but on five different occasions during the time he stayed with Dora someone tried the back screen. The first time Tommy was scared. He grabbed the shotgun and yelled, and the man ran. It was the same after that except he wasn't scared again.

"They're sneak thieves," Ben Lampe said. "They go around trying the back doors of the business houses, and if somebody forgets to lock the door, he gets

robbed. Bums, most of them. If Dora wasn't living on Main Street, I wouldn't worry about her. Trouble is, one of them bastards might get inside and then find out a woman was sleeping in the back of her shop. It could be damned serious."

Tommy had a feeling Lampe was worrying about more than sneak thieves, that it was Lampe's idea and not Dora's for Tommy to stay there, but he wasn't sure. Maybe Dora thought she could look out for herself. In any case, she never made Tommy feel uncomfortable. She accepted him, treating him as if he were a younger brother.

Lampe always had Sunday dinner with them, and supper on an average of twice a week. On those occasions Dora put a little extra on the table, but even on the ordinary days Tommy had no reason to complain about her cooking. He soon found out she hated to do dishes, and most of the time it fell to him to clean up the kitchen. But he didn't mind it. This was nothing compared to the housework he had done for Aunt Sadie.

As Lampe had told him, there was very little work for him to do. He saw that Dora had plenty of fuel, he swept and dusted the shop every morning before she opened up, and he persuaded her to buy a brush and paint and he painted the outside of the building, even though it was rented and Lampe considered the entire enterprise a waste of money.

Dora patched Tommy's clothes and bought him some new ones. On Sunday mornings she took him to

Sunday school and church, and introduced him to boys his age, but he didn't find any he particularly liked. On week days when he couldn't find anything to do, he often sat and talked to Dora while she worked on her hats. He learned she was an orphan who had been raised by an older sister who must, the way Dora described her, have been a mate to Aunt Sadie.

Dora had made her own way since she was fifteen, and she wasn't at all critical of Tommy for running away from Aunt Sadie. "I know exactly how you felt, even if I'm not a boy," she said. "You get a squeezed-in feeling, as if the walls are moving in against you."

That, Tommy thought, was exactly the way he had felt before he left Aunt Sadie's boarding house.

Dora didn't have much business and Tommy wondered how she made a living. He couldn't bring himself to ask her, although he did learn that Ben Lampe paid the rent on her building. Beyond that she never volunteered any information about her present life in Winnemucca or her business or even where she had come from. All he found out was that she was twenty-one and had been here two years. She didn't tell him, either, why she didn't marry Lampe, although it was plain enough the marshal was in love with her.

Tommy wandered around town in the afternoons, spending most of his time in the livery stables and asking about jobs, because Dora had told him she wouldn't keep him past November. If he didn't find something by then he'd be worse off than when he'd come to Winnemucca, because winter would be close.

He succeeded in hanging onto the eight dollars he'd had, and even added to it by doing odd jobs or running errands for people. He was liked by the business men, Ben Lampe told him. Still, he couldn't get a job, either in town or on one of the ranches nearby, and as August wore into September he had to fight the panic that began to crowd him.

Lampe kept telling him something would turn up. Maybe when cattle were driven to Winnemucca in the fall to be shipped out on the railroad. Some of the biggest herds came from Oregon, and he repeatedly heard the name of Mike Dugan who owned the Bar D far to the north of Quinn River and the Black Rock Desert.

The talk was that every fall Dugan brought the biggest steers that were shipped out of Winnemucca, that there were always buyers from San Francisco who bid against each other for the Bar D cattle and Dugan invariably got a premium price for his stock. He'd driven a herd north from California when he was hardly more than a boy, a liveryman named Alec Thorne told Tommy, and had settled on Frying Pan Creek west of the Two Medicine Peaks in south-eastern Oregon in the days when the country was wide open.

Dugan had made a fortune, partly because he was smart and worked hard and had picked a choice site for a ranch, and partly because the grass was good and in the more severe Oregon climate the cattle were free of diseases that were common on the warmer California ranges.

So, as the days passed, Tommy heard more and more of Mike Dugan and the Bar D, and he built up a mental picture of the man as a big swashbuckling cowman, the kind of man Tommy wanted to be. He told himself he'd get a job with Dugan. The Bar D outfit always stayed in town a week or so, and Ben Lampe had his hands full because Dugan's buckaroos thought they owned the earth and the moon and everything else.

When Tommy asked Lampe about Dugan, he was surprised at the way the marshal tightened up and got red in the face. "He's a wild Irishman," Lampe said. "Don't count on him for anything. He wouldn't give you the time of day."

Tommy didn't mention Dugan to Lampe again. Or to Dora, either, not supposing she would know him.

Lampe gave Tommy every moment he could spare. He usually didn't go on duty until noon, and then stayed on until midnight. When Dora didn't need Tommy, Lampe often came around with an extra horse and took Tommy into the country. He taught Tommy many things he needed to know, the basic facts about horses and ropes and guns, particularly guns, and coached him on the various situations he might run into, such as getting lost in the desert or in timber, and how to read sign.

"It's a hard land," Lampe said, "and you learn to hold what you have or somebody takes it away from you. We try to build respect for law, and we will in time, but the truth is that a gun is too often more of the law of the land than all the statutes they put on the books in the state capital."

He gave Tommy a .44 Colt, a holster and belt, and he spent at least two mornings a week in the country teaching Tommy to draw and fire, and impressed on him that accuracy was far more important than speed.

"I'm not fast," Lampe said. "No amount of practice will make me fast, but I shoot straight. I never get into a gun fight if I can avoid it, but if I'm jockeyed into one, I'll kill the man I'm drawing on if I can. The best advice I can give you is never to draw your gun on a man you don't aim to kill."

Dora didn't like it, and she told Lampe so one evening at supper. "He's sixteen," Lampe said. "He's as big as a man, and in this country that makes him a man. Winnemucca will be jumping in a couple of weeks when the herds get in, and I aim to teach Tommy to take care of himself."

"He doesn't have to be on the streets," Dora said tartly. "He can stay here with me."

Lampe gave her a look Tommy didn't understand. He said, "I'd like for him to stay here with you, but that's too much to ask with all the excitement we'll have going on around here." He paused, then added, "He may need to be able to take care of you and himself, too."

Dora's face turned bright red and she stared at her plate. They both dropped the matter then, but there was an undercurrent of uneasiness that bothered Tommy through the rest of the meal.

As soon as Lampe finished eating he left. That was unusual, for he ordinarily sat and talked until dark when it was time for him to start making his rounds. But again it was something Tommy didn't think he should ask about, and Dora offered no explanation.

Ben Lampe was not the kind of law man Tommy had read about in the Wild West stories he used to get hold of occasionally. Lampe wasn't a showoff. He moved slowly, he was good-natured, and could take a practical joke as well as give one, and Tommy learned the first week he was in Winnemucca that Ben Lampe was one of the most respected men in town.

Thorne, the liveryman, told Tommy: "Ben never loses his head. He can go into a crowded saloon when the trail crews are in town, bust up a fight, crack a few heads together, and haul a couple of drunk buckaroos off to jail. He's got plenty of sand in his craw, too. I've seen him stand up to some gunslick who's trying to make a name for himself, let the other fellow get in the first two shots and then drill him right between the eyes."

So Tommy watched and learned, thankful that Ben Lampe thought enough of him to try to teach him what he needed to know. He began to have more confidence in himself, certain that he'd make out, that he was a man, or nearly one.

chapter 3

THE HERDS BEGAN TRICKLING IN, the small ones at first, the big outfits from farther away coming later, and as Ben Lampe had said, the town was jumping. Tommy hung around the shipping pens every spare minute he had, for the action focused here and to him the excitement was as great one day as the next.

The bed grounds were in the valley along the river. From there the cattle were driven to the tracks as cars became available. A constant haze of dust hung over the shipping pens. Buyers from the coast haggled with the cowmen. Sometimes a horse trade was made. Now and then a fight broke out. There was always a lot of racket along the tracks with cars shunted around and trains made up, and always the prodding and cursing and shouting as the loading went on day after day.

But Mike Dugan and his Bar D didn't show up. When Tommy asked Alec Thorne about it, the liveryman said, "He'll be the last to get here. His outfit will take the town over, and Ben will have half of 'em in jail after they finish loading." He looked at Tommy closely, then asked, "Ben ever say anything to you about Dugan?"

"No."

Thorne sighed. "There'll come a day when one of 'em will kill the other one. Or they'll kill each other."

"Why?"

Thorne turned away. "Some men don't like each other. That's all."

"There must be a reason."

Thorne picked up a pitchfork and walked along the runway. Then he stopped and looked back. "Dugan don't like the way Ben throws the Bar D buckaroos into the jug when they start raising hell. Don't you say nothing to Ben about this. You mind now."

"Sure," Tommy said, but he still wasn't satisfied with Thorne's answer.

He asked Dora about it that night and immediately wished he hadn't. She gave him an inquiring glance as if trying to probe his mind to see if there was anything behind the question. Then she said, "It's like Thorne told you. Ben won't let the Bar D men tear the town up."

Tommy didn't think any more about it until the day that a great cloud of dust appeared to the north, and the rumor spread along Bridge Street that the Bar D bunch would be in town by night. Tommy was with Ben Lampe at the shipping pens that afternoon when Mike Dugan rode up.

Tommy pegged the man as being Dugan long before he stepped out of the saddle. He rode a big black gelding, his saddle the most ornate and probably the most expensive one Tommy had ever seen in his life. He rode well, gracefully and easily, carrying most of his weight in the stirrups. From the waist up he swayed with each movement of his horse; from the waist down he moved with the horse's body. When he saw Lampe, he gave him a bare, quarter-inch nod, then he stepped down.

Now that he was on the ground, Tommy saw that he was big, bigger even than Ben Lampe, taller and certainly wider of shoulder, tapering to a slender waist so that he was roughly shaped like a triangle. Bright red hair that needed trimming showed under the brim of his sweat-stained hat, and his sweeping mustache was as red as his hair. His features were rough, dominated by a big nose and a square chin. No beauty, Tommy thought, and yet there was a masculine handsomeness about him that stemmed from the very roughness of his features.

"Howdy, Lampe," Dugan said.

"Howdy, Dugan," Lampe said.

Neither offered to shake hands. Each pair of eyes raked the other, eyes that showed grudging respect. They were like two great dogs, hackles up, ready to spring at the other's throat at the first provocation.

"The herd'll be in tonight," Dugan said.

"Good," Lampe said. "You'll be leaving town in about three days, then."

"Not quite that soon," Dugan said. "The boys'll want to blow off a little steam."

"Keep 'em in line," Lampe said.

"They'll stay in line."

"Or they'll be in jail."

Dugan shrugged. "Then I'll pay their fines. Your Goddamned town wouldn't be solvent if we didn't show up once a year."

He started past Lampe, then paused when Tommy said, "I'm Tommy Gordon. I need a job. Can you give me one?"

26

Dugan looked as if he had been insulted. He brushed past Tommy, shoving him out of the way with a thrust of his big hand, and strode on toward the tracks, his spurs jingling.

Tommy stared at his back, hating him. Lampe said, "I told you he wouldn't give you the time of day."

"I've got to have a job," Tommy said miserably.

"There have been other outfits here," Lampe said. "You didn't ask none for jobs."

"I had a notion I wanted to work for Dugan," Tommy said.

"And a damn fool notion it was," Lampe said sourly. "It's not just a case of a big cattleman swallowing up his little neighbors, which I hear he does. It's more of a proposition of him swallowing everything and everybody. He's even got the town treed."

Lampe scratched the back of his neck, eyes on Dugan, who had stopped to talk to a couple of buyers from San Francisco, then he laid a hand on Tommy's shoulder. "I want you to promise me something. There'll be hell to pay around here till he gets his crew out of town. I don't want you to leave Dora's place at night for anything. From the time you eat supper, you stay right there with her."

Tommy didn't understand, for Lampe hadn't been concerned about the other outfits that had hit town, but Tommy had learned never to question the marshal when he gave an order. "All right, Ben," Tommy said.

When he went into Dora's kitchen that night, he found Mike Dugan there, shaved, bathed, in clean

27

clothes and with a haircut. Dora was frying steak at the stove. She said, "Mike, I want you to meet Tommy Gordon. He's been staying with me this summer."

Dugan gave him the short, arrogant nod which seemed to be typical of him. "Howdy, Gordon," he said.

Tommy's resentment boiled over. He turned his back to Dugan as he faced Dora. "I didn't know you knew him."

"Oh, Mike and I are old friends," she said lightly.

"I asked him for a job," Tommy said. "He didn't even answer me. He just gave me a push and went on."

Dora glanced at Dugan, trying to smile, and brought her gaze quickly back to her meat. "That wasn't very polite, was it, Tommy?"

"It was worse'n that." Tommy resented Dugan's presence here and he sensed that Dugan resented his, and suddenly he was reckless. "All summer I've heard what a big man he was and I figured he was the one I wanted to work for." He swung around and faced Dugan. "I didn't ask any of the other outfits for jobs, but I sure made a mistake."

Dugan laughed a great laugh and slapped his leg. "Your little friend's got spunk, Dora."

"You might reconsider, Mike," Dora said. "Tommy's a good boy and he's a hard worker."

"Sure, I'll reconsider," Dugan said, but Tommy knew he wouldn't.

"Wash up, Tommy," Dora said. "Supper's almost ready."

Tommy turned to the sink, washed his hands and face, combed his hair, and going to the table, sat down. There was no talk as they ate, Dora embarrassed and uneasy, Dugan ignoring Tommy completely, and Tommy, for the first time since he had come here, finding it hard to eat.

When the meal was finished Dugan leaned back, his amused eyes on Tommy. He tossed a ten-dollar gold piece on the table. "Go have yourself a good time, kid. Get drunk or sit in on a poker game."

Tommy scooted his chair back against the wall and sat with his hands on his knees. "I'm staying right here."

Dugan wasn't amused now. He rose, his big hands forming fists at his sides. Dora said, "Mike." He stood glaring at Tommy, then Dora said, "No, Mike."

He turned to her. "Let your dishes go."

She nodded. "I'll get my sweater."

Dugan walked to the stove and stood there as he took a cigar from his pocket, bit off the end, and lighted it. Tommy stared at Dugan's back, not wanting Dora to go but knowing he couldn't stop her. Ben Lampe had said for him to stay here and that was all he could do.

A moment later Dora came out of her bedroom. "You go on to bed when you're ready, Tommy," she said. "I don't know when I'll be back."

He nodded, and remained there as Dora went out through the back door and across the porch, Dugan following. The screen door banged shut. A cowboy pounded down Bridge Street, letting out a high yell and firing his gun a couple of times. A dog barked, then howled shrilly when someone kicked him out of the way.

Tommy sat there a long time, disturbed because he thought Ben Lampe would blame him for letting Dora go, but what could he have done? He got up finally and cleared the table, leaving the gold piece where Dugan had left it.

Tommy stayed up, the hours dragging, the town gradually becoming quiet. He finally went to sleep, his head tipping forward, waking sometime after midnight when Dora came in. He rubbed his eyes and looked at Dora, who stood across the table regarding him with questioning eyes. Her hair was mussed, her cheeks were very bright, and she had an expression of airy happiness on her face Tommy had never seen before.

She came to the table and put an arm around Tommy's shoulder and hugged him. "I told you to go to bed," she said.

"I was worried," he said. "I didn't want you to go."

"I was all right. You're a good boy, Tommy. Ben didn't make any mistake about you." She hesitated, then added, "I want you to promise me something, Tommy. Don't tell Ben I was gone tonight."

He was uneasy. Lampe had extracted one promise from him, and now Dora wanted another. He couldn't say no. He guessed he couldn't say no to anything Dora asked. He said, "I promise."

30

She kissed him on the cheek. "Don't worry if Mike doesn't give you that job you wanted. We'll work something out. Go to bed now."

He did, but the uneasiness lingered in him as he wondered where she had gone and what she had done. Again it was something he couldn't ask her.

chapter 4

BAR D WAS IN TOWN FOR A WEEK. Tommy spent all of his spare time around the shipping pens, most of it with Ben Lampe. He didn't tell Lampe about Dugan being at Dora's for supper and about her leaving with him. As far as Tommy knew, Dugan hadn't been back since that first night, but Dora was gone every evening. She didn't say where she went and Tommy didn't ask, but he had a hunch she was with Dugan. That was something else he didn't mention to Ben Lampe.

Tommy soon learned to recognize most of the Bar D crew. There was the big vaquero, Pablo Garcia, who, Alec Thorne told Tommy, had helped drive Dugan's first herd into Oregon and who had been with him ever since. There was Todd Moody, a freckle-faced buckaroo who wasn't over twenty but was one of the best hands Dugan had, according to Lampe. And there was Lew Roman, Dugan's foreman, with a face that had been scorched a bright red and a booming voice that could be heard above the bellowing of the cattle.

There were others, ten or twelve all together, but the

31

only one who knew that Tommy Gordon existed was Bert Mayer. He stopped and talked to Lampe occasionally and so knew who Tommy was. Several times Tommy ran into him at Alec Thorne's livery stable and Mayer always had time to visit.

Mayer was older than most of Dugan's crew, about forty, Tommy thought, although he might not have been that old because he had a white mustache that added years to his appearance. His brows were thick and long and black, and when he took off his hat, Tommy discovered he was completely bald. He was tall and very thin, with a lean, deeply lined face that held a melancholy expression which bothered Tommy. Mayer seldom joked or laughed the way the others did, but he was always friendly, with none of the arrogance that characterized Dugan and most of his men.

On the day Bar D finished loading Tommy asked Ben Lampe about Mayer. "He's a queer one," Lampe said, shaking his head. "Most of the time he's easygoing and quiet like, but when it comes to a fight, he's cold turkey. I've seen him kill two men and he didn't turn a hair. Wasn't his fault, so I didn't arrest him."

"He doesn't act like he belongs to the crew," Tommy said. "I've watched him. If he isn't working, he's alone."

Lampe nodded. "I guess he's not really a Bar D man. He's got a little spread out in the desert, they tell me. The Lazy K. It's a kind of partnership with Dugan, and there's always a shirttailful of Lazy K steers with the Bar D herd." Lampe filled his pipe, glancing obliquely at Tommy. "The part I don't savvy is that he hates Dugan. If I hated a man, I sure as hell wouldn't stay partners with him."

"They ever fight?"

"No. Fact is, nobody ever told me that Mayer hates Dugan, but after you pack a star for a while, you get a feeling for things like that." Lampe filled his pipe and pulled on it, then added, "There's a dozen men right here in Winnemucca who hate Dugan enough to kill him, but nobody ever tries it. You're either like Lew Roman and Todd Moody, thinking Dugan's one notch higher'n God, or you figure he's the devil like Mayer does. There's nothing halfway about Mike Dugan."

"I guess you hate him," Tommy said.

Lampe gave him a wry grin. "Sure I do. Same as almost everybody else in Winnemucca. Mostly it's because he's got a way of walking over us like we're dirt. I've been waiting a long time for him to make a wrong move, but he never does." Lampe tamped the tobacco a little tighter into the bowl of his pipe, then added, "But that don't explain Bert Mayer."

At supper that night Tommy asked Dora about Mayer, but she shrugged her shoulders. "I don't know, but Ben might be wrong. Just because he doesn't like Mike doesn't prove that other people hate him."

When they finished eating, Dora went into her bedroom, stayed there a good five minutes, and came out wearing her sweater and smelling of the lilac perfume she kept on her dresser. She dropped an arm over Tommy's shoulder as she had been doing a good deal lately, and said, "I don't think you'd like working for Mike, Tommy. If you don't find something else, you can stay here with me."

"You said you couldn't keep me after November."

"I've changed my mind," she said, and walked to the back door.

"Don't go, Dora," he said.

She turned with her hand on the knob and smiled at him. "I'll be all right."

"Let me walk with you," he urged. "Ben would skin me if anything happened to you."

"Nothing will happen to me," she said.

She went out, closing the door behind her. He heard her cross the back porch, heard the screen slam shut, and then she was gone. He had no idea where she planned to go, but he supposed she was with Mike Dugan until Ben Lampe came an hour later.

"Where's Dora?" Lampe asked.

"I don't know," Tommy answered. "She left right after supper. She didn't say anything about where she was going."

"Why didn't you follow her?"

"You told me to stay here."

"Yeah, I guess I did." Lampe stood in the kitchen looking around the room, his face gray, a pulse throbbing in his forehead. Then he said, "I don't get it. Dugan's playing poker in Callahan's Bar." He turned to the door, then looked back at Tommy. "We can't do anything for Dora, looks like. You might as well go out and see the fun. There'll be some, if Bar D rides out in the morning. If they lay over another day, the fun will be tomorrow night." His grin lay tight across his mouth. "The fun won't amount to much, though. I'll see to that."

Lampe went out. Tommy hesitated, vaguely disturbed, although he wasn't sure why. He'd felt that way ever since Mike Dugan had come to town. The dishes were done, so there was no reason for him to stay here. He got his hat and put on his coat, and went out into the cold night.

Bridge Street was quiet enough. Tommy reached Callahan's Bar and paused to look through the window. Dugan was playing poker. So were most of his boys, but Lew Roman stood at the bar arguing with another buckaroo in a loud voice. Drunk, Tommy thought. Ben Lampe would have his fun tonight.

Tommy went on toward the hotel, walking slowly, still uneasy. Dora's behavior all week bothered him. It wasn't like her and he didn't understand it. He remembered how good Dora had been to him and how panicky he had been the first day he'd come to Winnemucca and couldn't find work. He didn't know what would have happened to him if she hadn't given him a place to stay.

He saw Ben Lampe sitting in front of the hotel on a bench. Tommy sat down beside Lampe, asking, "What are you doing?"

"Waiting," Lampe answered. "Bar D's riding out in the morning."

Silence for a moment, and then because Tommy

couldn't stop worrying about Dora, he said, "Why don't you marry Dora, Ben?"

Lampe didn't say anything. He stared into the darkness, then turned to look at Tommy, the light from the hotel window falling across his face that was as gray as it had been in Dora's kitchen.

"I'll never marry her," he said thickly.

Tommy hesitated, his uneasiness growing. Then he said, "Dora told me I can stay with her this winter."

"It wouldn't work. Have you asked Bert Mayer for a job?"

"No."

"He's in Thorne's livery stable. Go ask him. He can't pay you much, but you'll have a place to stay, and he'll teach you things I couldn't."

Still Tommy sat there. Finally he said, "I'm sure worried about Dora. I wish I knew where she was."

"You hear what I said?" Lampe asked harshly. "About Mayer?"

"Yeah, I heard."

"Well, go on. Ask him. He's riding out tonight."

Tommy got up and walked on toward the stable, not understanding the note of urgency that had been in Lampe's voice. He found Mayer talking to Alec Thorne in Thorne's office. He paused in the doorway, not sure he should interrupt, but Mayer glanced up and gave him his slow smile.

"Come in, Tommy," Mayer said.

"I've been looking for a job," Tommy said. "Ben said you might have one for me."

"I might," Mayer said. "I hear you asked Mike and he just pushed you out of his way and kept going."

"He sure did," Tommy said. "Dora said she guessed I wouldn't want to work for Dugan."

"Oh, I don't know," Mayer said. "He's got a big outfit. He could use a chore boy."

"I'm not going to ask him again," Tommy said.

Mayer held a cigar in his right hand. Now he rolled it between thumb and forefinger, looking down at it. He said, "Well, I can give you a job. Trouble is, I can't offer you much. A bed in the attic and your meals and five dollars a month. I'll find you a horse and saddle if that'll help."

"I'll take it," Tommy said eagerly. "I'd take it without the five dollars if you can't afford to pay it."

"Never undercut a man's offer, son," Thorne advised.

"That's right," Mayer said. "I reckon I can afford it, but I'd better tell you I don't have a wife. I have a daughter about your age who keeps house for me, a boy thirteen, and a year-old baby. Our house ain't much and our grub ain't fancy, but I'd like to have you work for me. How about it?"

"You haven't said anything to change my mind," Tommy said.

"All right," Mayer said. "I figure to get started in half an hour. Go pack up anything you've got and get back here. I'll have a horse for you."

"I want to tell Dora good-by," Tommy said. "She isn't home and I don't know when she'll be back."

Mayer and Thorne exchanged glances, then Thorne said, "Write her a note, son."

"It's a long ride," Mayer said. "We'd better get started."

"I guess I could write her a note," Tommy said, "but I'd sure like to see her. . . ."

"Go on," Thorne said. "She'll understand."

He had the same tone of urgency in his voice that Tommy had heard in Ben Lampe's a few minutes before. Tommy didn't understand it, but he caught no clue of what was in Thorne's mind in the expression on the liveryman's face.

"All right," Tommy said. "I'll be right back."

He ran to the millinery shop, found an empty flour sack and stuffed his clothes into it. He stood looking around, reluctant to leave.

Then he remembered the note, found pencil and paper, and wrote: "I'm leaving tonight with Bert Mayer. He's going to give me a job. I wanted to tell you good-by, but I didn't know where you were." He paused, thinking of so many things he wanted to say, and couldn't. So he added, "Thanks for taking care of me. Tommy."

He blew out the lamp and went out through the front. When he approached Callahan's bar, he saw Lampe come out with Lew Roman, who was staggering as if he were drunk, a trickle of blood flowing down his face from a scalp wound. Tommy followed them, wanting to tell Lampe good-by, but knowing this was no time to talk to him.

38

Tommy kept his distance until Lampe reached the jail. He waited in front until Lampe came out. He said, "Mayer's giving me a job. I'm leaving with him right away."

He held out his hand and Lampe took it, giving Tommy only part of his attention, his gaze searching the darkness. Lampe said, "Good luck, boy."

"Thanks for everything you've done for me," Tommy said.

"Glad to." Lampe gave him a shove toward the stable. "Don't keep Mayer waiting."

"Dora's not home yet," Tommy said, "so I left a note."

"She'll understand." Lampe stiffened, his eyes on the lighted area in front of the hotel. "Mayer's waiting." He gave Tommy another shove, a harder one this time. "Go on."

Something was wrong. This wasn't like Lampe. Tommy stood motionless, his heart pounding as the conviction that something was wrong grew in him. Lampe said harshly, "Damn it, go on! What have I got to do to you to get you off the street?"

Tommy backed away into the darkness, then he saw that Mike Dugan was walking toward the jail in slow, deliberate steps. Tommy didn't know where he had come from. Maybe from the hotel. Or Callahan's Bar which was on beyond the hotel.

Lampe didn't move. When Dugan was ten feet away, Lampe said, "You can stop right there, Mike. What's on your mind?"

Dugan stopped, his big hands shoved into his belt,

gaze raking Lampe's face, a contemptuous smile on his lips. "Did you have to pistol whip Lew?"

"He resisted arrest," Lampe said. "I should have killed him."

"You know what would have happened if you had?"

"I know what you would have tried."

"And we'd have done it. I think this is your last year here, marshal. Winnemucca needs my business more than it needs your services."

"That may be," Lampe said, "but right now I'm marshal."

"I'll have Lew out in the morning," Dugan said, and walked away.

Lampe stood watching until Dugan disappeared into the hotel, then Tommy heard him curse in a tone be had never heard before, a tone filled with so much hatred that it terrified Tommy.

Ten minutes later Tommy was riding north through the darkness with Bert Mayer, still not understanding what had happened to Ben Lampe. When he told Mayer about it, Mayer only said, "He was angry, Tommy."

But that was no explanation. Tommy had seen Lampe angry before, but he had never heard him curse as he had tonight. There was more to it, Tommy thought, much more that he didn't understand.

chapter 5

TOMMY RODE NORTH with Bert Mayer under a clear
sky with its cold half moon and bright pattern of stars.
Sometime, long after midnight, Mayer pulled up,
saying they would sleep a couple of hours. But
Tommy couldn't sleep. He lay on the ground and
stared at the black ceiling of the sky, his head on his
saddle, the saddle blanket over him, and thought of
what happened in Winnemucca, of Ben Lampe and
Dora Lind, and Mike Dugan.

He still didn't understand it, and it puzzled and worried him. He didn't understand Mayer, either, who lay
snoring in the sagebrush a few feet from him, or why
Mayer had bothered with him.

Then his thoughts turned to the future. This was a
hilltop in his life, with a fog-shrouded valley before
him. There had been many such hilltops in the past.
When his folks had died and Aunt Sadie had taken
him to Nebraska. When he had walked out of Aunt
Sadie's house and boarded the train. When he'd got
off at Winnemucca and walked Bridge Street all
morning searching for a job, and finally had been
taken in by Dora Lind.

But now all that was behind him and he was heading
into the unknown again with Bert Mayer. He raised a
hand to feel of the peach fuzz that had begun to give
his face a dirty appearance no matter how hard he
scrubbed, of the pimple that was a red splotch on his

chin. The cold seeped in under his blanket and he drew his hand back and tucked the blanket under him.

He felt as if he were something old and battered that had been rolled along through space by the wind of destiny, stopping here and there when the wind died, only to be picked up by the wind again and hurled through space. Suddenly he wanted to cry, but he couldn't. Crying was for children, and he wasn't a child any more.

He heard a coyote give voice to his loneliness from a rim to the north; he heard some tiny desert animal rustle the dry grass as it raced from one hiding place to another a few feet from his head. Then the moon died below the western horizon, and the stars slowly faded as the opalescent dawn light began touching the eastern sky.

Suddenly the loneliness was in him, too. It was in the wind that rattled the sage brush and pelted each bush with sand; it was in the slithering sound of the night animal that rushed to another hiding place, always seeking and always fearful and therefore never quite finding the perfection that it sought. It was in the tangy incense of the desert; it was in the wildness and massiveness of the empty land that pressed against him, and suddenly the unbidden tears came.

Mayer woke as suddenly as if an invisible alarm clock inside his brain had spurred it into life. He called, "Rustle some wood, Tommy, and I'll fix a bit of breakfast."

Tommy turned his face from Mayer, wiping a sleeve

across his eyes. He got up, knowing he hadn't slept, tired and so sore from the hours of riding that he could hardly walk, but he didn't complain. He couldn't, he knew, and hold Bert Mayer's respect, and right now that was the thing he must do above everything else.

Later he huddled over the fire, shivering, and wolfed down his breakfast, not realizing he was ravenously hungry until he smelled the coffee. They lingered a moment, Mayer rolling a cigarette and lighting it with a flaming twig. For some reason Tommy thought of Mike Dugan again, then of Ben Lampe and Dora Lind, and he asked, "What kind of man is Mike Dugan?"

Mayer looked up, frowning, and took the cigarette out of his mouth. He had an old, young face, weathered until it was deeply lined and burned to the color of aged leather.

"Hard to tell you," Mayer said finally. "Maybe you'd savvy if I said he was like a fast freight, highballing along and not paying no heed to the signals beside the track."

He paused, staring down at the cigarette that had gone cold in his fingers, then he added, "Or maybe it would be plainer if I said he was the kind of man who wouldn't have anyone to cry for him if he died tomorrow unless it was his girl Bonnie. She's eleven and he always brings her presents when he's been gone."

Mayer thought a moment, then he said thoughtfully, "We're all just a little wink on the face of eternity,

43

then we're gone. If there's no one who gives a good Goddamn about you, then you're not very much." He rose and threw his cigarette into the fire. "Time we were riding."

The sun was a red rind above the eastern horizon when they rode north, later angling toward the west. Presently a mountain range appeared ahead of them, and Mayer said, "That's the Two Medicine Peaks range. The high ridge you see yonder is South Medicine." He pointed to a cluster of buildings far to the east. "That's Barney Coombs's roadhouse. Likely Dugan and his boys will stay the night there and get to the Bar D tomorrow."

Silence again that ran on hour after hour. Dozens of questions crossed Tommy's mind. Were they in Oregon yet? Were they on Bar D range? Was it all like this desert?

But he did not voice any of the questions that occurred to him. A dark expression had settled upon Mayer's melancholy face that forbade it. Not an unfriendly or hostile one, but rather one which told Tommy that the man was lost in private thoughts and problems he could not share.

In midafternoon they entered a narrow valley threaded by a meandering stream which was flanked by close-growing willows. Rimrock walled the valley on both sides, with here and there an occasional break. Tommy remembered Ben Lampe telling him how cowmen fenced breaks in the rimrock and so controlled thousands of acres of grass that did not belong to them. Dugan and a few powerful neighbors had used this method to seize and hold their empires, with the result that a vast area of public domain which was legally open to entry was actually not open at all.

Mayer pointed to the creek. "It's running low now. You'll catch some of the biggest trout you ever seen in the riffles and you'll wonder how they keep their bellies wet without drying off their backs. Most years we have considerable snow. When we do, the creek flows all over the whole valley come spring, and then Dugan has all the hay he needs. Cheapest and best irrigation in the world."

"What's the name of the creek?" Tommy asked.

"Dugan named it the Frying Pan," Mayer answered. "He was the first one to settle hereabouts, and he found an old rusty frying pan a mile or so above his buildings. Nobody knows where it came from. Maybe Fremont and Kit Carson went through here and left it."

Mayer lapsed into silence again. The valley widened as they rode north, with small streams coming in from the mountains to the east. As little as Tommy knew about the cattle country, he recognized this for the fine grassland that it was. There was probably desert to the west, and on the east the Two Medicine Peaks range rose in long slopes above the rimrock, but here in the valley was the graze that gave the Bar D cattle their reputation.

Darkness had settled down upon the valley before they reached the Bar D, the lights in the windows of the ranch house and bunk house and cook shack beckoning to them long before they arrived.

As they reined up Mayer said, "You'd be better off here working for Dugan than going on with me to the Lazy K. It's not that I wouldn't like to have you, but there's a future here and there's none with me on the Lazy K. I've got an idea I'm going to work on. Just play along and don't open the corral gate at the wrong time."

That was all. It gave a puzzling turn to Tommy's thinking, for he would have been glad to have a place to spend the winter, future or no future. But he trusted Bert Mayer, so he didn't argue.

An old man drifted out of the darkness and took the reins as Mayer and Tommy stepped down. "Mike ain't with you?" the old man asked.

"No," Mayer answered. "He'll probably be in tomorrow night."

Mayer turned toward the house, passing through a row of poplar trees that were tall and ghostly in the moonlight. When Tommy caught up with him he said, "The biggest ranch in the country. The best steers year after year. The house the showplace of this corner of the state. The fastest racehorses anywhere around. All in a little over ten years. You've got to give the devil his due."

Then, just before they reached the porch which ran the full width of the house, Mayer said, "Don't ask about Bonnie's mother. She left Dugan when Bonnie was five. Bonnie thinks she's dead, and maybe she is. Dugan's sister Rose keeps house for him."

Mayer went in without knocking, closing the door behind Tommy, and called, "Rose." He left his Stetson on a hall tree, indicating for Tommy to do the same, and stepped into the parlor.

Tommy followed, but he stopped one step past the door, not expecting luxury like this. High-piled carpet under his feet, heavy dark furniture, a shiny piano against one wall, a huge fireplace at the far end with a dozen brands burned into the mantel, and tall gold candlesticks on the center table.

A girl ran into the room, blonde and blue-eyed and chubby. She cried, "Bert," and ran to him. He picked her up and held her high while she kicked and squealed, then he hugged her and put her down.

"Your dad will be along tomorrow night, I think," Mayer said. "I came on ahead with Tommy Gordon. Tommy, this is Bonnie Dugan."

Bonnie turned to him, smiling. "How do you do, Tommy."

She was composed, being neither too forward nor too bashful. "I'm pleased to meet you," he mumbled, and remained by the door, embarrassed because he suddenly became aware of his big hands and big feet, and the pimple on his chin.

A tall woman came into the room and gave her hand to Mayer, asking, "How was Winnemucca, Bert?"

"The same, Rose," Mayer said, and nodded at Tommy. "I brought a partner along. Miss Dugan, meet Tommy Gordon."

She walked to Tommy, her hand extended, a graceful woman who didn't look over twenty-five, and yet somehow seemed older, perhaps because of her dignity. She had rich auburn hair which she wore in a high crown on her head; her features were regular, showing no resemblance to the rugged face of her brother.

"I'm happy to meet you, Tommy," she said, and turned back to Mayer as Tommy mumbled something. "We've had our supper, but there's pie left. I'll heat up the coffee and fry some bacon and eggs for you."

"Don't bother, Rose," Mayer said. "We'll get Ah Wing to fix us something."

"He'll take a butcher knife to you," Rose said. "You know how he is if you're late for a meal. Come on back to the kitchen. I want to hear about the drive."

Mayer winked at Tommy. "No use arguing with her. It just don't pay."

chapter 6

TOMMY FOLLOWED MAYER through the dining room with it's cherrywood table covered by a damask cloth and the big sideboard set against the wall, and on into the kitchen. Here Tommy felt at home, for the kitchen was very much like the one at Aunt Sadie's, a long room with a table in the center covered by a red-and-white checked oilcloth, a big range with a door beyond it leading into the pantry, and a pump and sink close to the wall across from the stove.

Mayer and Tommy washed while Rose moved the coffee pot to the front of the stove. Turning, she disappeared into the pantry for the ham and eggs. Bonnie set two places at the table, then took a chair at the end and lacing her fingers, dropped her chin upon them and regarded Tommy with a solemn gaze.

Rose filled the fire box, saying angrily, "I don't have any wood for breakfast. You'll have to light the lantern and cut some, Bert. That Ole Crabbe gets lazier all the time. I told Mike just before he left that he was going to go hungry one of these days."

Mayer nodded at a lantern hanging near the back door. "Fetch in some wood, Tommy. Bonnie can show you where the woodpile is."

"Slip on your sweater, Bonnie," Rose said. "It's real chilly tonight."

Carrying the lantern, Tommy followed Bonnie across the porch to the pile of logs. As he set the lantern beside the chopping block, Bonnie said, "Ole sawed a lot of wood today, so all you've got to do is to split some. Rose says Ole's lazy, but he isn't. He's just got too much to do."

As Tommy picked up a chunk and split it with a single blow of the ax, Bonnie went on, "Ole's the old man who took your horses when you got here. He helped daddy drive his first herd to the Frying Pan when he started the Bar D. He's the only one that's left besides Lew Roman and Pablo Garcia. Ole's got rheumatism. That's why he's so slow."

She'd talk a man to death, Tommy thought as he

49

picked up another chunk and split it.

"You're strong, Tommy," Bonnie said. "How old are you?"

"Sixteen."

"You're big for your age. Where did you come from?"

"Nebraska."

"That's a long ways off, isn't it?"

"Yes."

He worked as fast as he could, but he was tired and stiff, and it seemed the ax wouldn't land where he aimed. Then he struck a perverse knot that held him up, and all the time Bonnie was talking, asking questions and not giving him time to answer.

"You better go inside," he said. "You're getting cold."

She was shivering, but she shook her head. "No, I'm not."

As soon as he had an armload of wood, he stuck the ax into the chopping block and picked up the wood. "I'll take the lantern," she said, and marched ahead of him, carefully holding the lantern so he wouldn't stumble. He dropped the wood into the box, took the lantern from Bonnie, and blowing it out, hung it on the nail beside the door.

Rose was standing at the stove. She said, "Bert told me about how you lost your parents. I'm sorry, Tommy."

He blinked at her, surprised that Mayer knew about it. Tommy hadn't mentioned it on the trip north. Ben Lampe must have told him.

"Bert says you need a job for the winter," Rose went on. "How would you like to stay here? Do chores for me like cutting wood. Looking out for Bonnie when she goes riding. She has a pony and a cart, but she doesn't get to ride very much. None of the buckaroos have time to harness up for her."

Tommy looked at her and then at Mayer. He swallowed, thinking that Bonnie would drive him crazy with her chatter. Rose went on, "I don't know how much we can pay you, but I'll talk to Mike about it as soon as he gets here."

"Say yes, Tommy," Bonnie cried. "Please say yes."

It occurred to Tommy that Mayer had never intended to take him to his own ranch. He squared his shoulders and met Rose's gaze. "I'm obliged, ma'am. I'll be glad to work here."

Rose smiled and motioned toward the table. "I'm glad, Tommy. Now you go sit down. These eggs are almost done."

He nearly fell asleep at the table after he'd eaten, and Mayer said, "You going to give him the back room, Rose?"

"Yes," Rose said. "Why don't you take him upstairs, Bert?"

Bonnie jumped to her feet. "I'll take him."

"You stay and help me," Rose said. "Bert knows which room it is."

Bonnie sat down, pouting. Mayer picked up a lamp from the table. "Come on, son, before you fall over in your tracks."

Tommy followed him into the hall and up the stairs to a small room in the back of the house. He dropped down on the bed, staring at Mayer and in that moment he thought he hated him. He said, "You didn't aim to take me to your place. You didn't want me."

Mayer looked down at him, his face more melancholy than ever. He said, "You got that wrong, boy. Rose has needed someone for a long time. She has to do things like chopping wood and tending garden, chores she shouldn't have to do. I thought I could work it this way, but it wasn't 'cause I didn't want you. I have a boy of my own, you know, so I didn't need you. Rose does."

He walked to the door as Tommy said, "Dugan will have a fit when he sees me."

Mayer turned. "Sure he will, but if anybody can get the best of him, Rose can. If it don't work out, you come to the Lazy K. I promised to give you a place to stay the winter, and if you need it, I will."

Mayer left the next morning. At dusk Dugan rode in with his crew. Rose kept Tommy in the back of the house when Dugan came in, his spurs jingling. He hugged and kissed Bonnie, then gave her the presents he had brought: a doll, a pink parasol, and a blue dress. He was sitting on the leather couch watching Bonnie play with her new doll when Rose took Tommy into the parlor with her.

"I'm glad you're back, Mike," Rose said. "Did you have a good trip?"

Dugan looked up, started to say something, and

stopped abruptly. Then he bellowed, "What'n hell is that Goddamned brat doing here?"

Rose stood at the end of the center table, a hand on Tommy's shoulder. Dugan's outburst did not ruffle her. She stood very straight, wearing her dignity like a shield. "Don't use that tone on me, and don't use those words in front of Bonnie. To answer your question, Tommy is working here."

"Working here?" Dugan looked at her stupidly as if dazed, his florid face as red as his hair, then he stood up. "Get him out of here. I don't know how in hell he got here, but get him out. He's not working for me."

Bonnie began to cry.

"I don't have to . . . ," Tommy began.

"Be quiet." Rose's hand shook his shoulder. "I know his story, Mike. I know that for weeks this summer he counted on getting a job here because he'd heard about you. I guess he thought you were something you weren't. When he asked you for a job, you didn't even answer him. You just walked off."

Dugan sat down again, glancing worriedly at Bonnie who had dropped her doll to the floor and was shaking with sobs. He wipe a big hand across his face as if he couldn't understand what was happening. He said, "Sure I walked off. I ain't hiring every bum who asks me for a job."

"I need someone to do chores around the house," Rose said evenly. "You keep promising me that Ole Crabbe is going to do them, but he doesn't. Bonnie needs someone to saddle a horse when she takes a ride, or harness her pony if she wants to use her cart. She needs someone to study with, someone for company."

"The hell she—"

"I'm not done. Listen, Mike. Listen carefully. If you send this boy on, you're sending me on. There are some things in the world besides buckets that you fill with gold and bury in your yard, things besides cows and swamps to clear and ditches to dig and settlers to push off land that rightfully is theirs. Things like raising an eleven-year-old daughter. Can you do them by yourself, Mike?"

He wiped a hand across his face again, a pulse beating in his temples. He turned to Bonnie and put an arm around her. He started to speak, choked, and cleared his throat, "You dropped your doll, honey."

"I don't want it," she said, and escaped his circling arm. "I want Tommy to stay here and you won't let him."

Dugan leaned back, head tipped forward to stare at the dusty toes of his boots. Watching him, Tommy thought that at last he was facing something he couldn't handle and it was hurting him with an agony he could not bear.

"All right," Dugan said at last. "He can stay."

"How much are you paying him?" Rose asked in the same even tone she had been using. "Bert offered him five dollars a month, but you can do better."

"Bert?" Dugan stared at Rose, then at Tommy. "So that's it. Yeah, I can do better. Ten dollars a month."

Tommy remembered the scene in Dora Lind's kitchen. Now this. It was too much. Mike Dugan would never forgive him. He would hate him, Tommy thought, as long as he lived.

chapter 7

MIKE DUGAN WAS AN EXPERT at ignoring anything or anybody whose presence he didn't want to recognize. It was that way with Tommy. To Dugan he simply did not exist. Dugan ate his meals in the house when he was home, which wasn't often because he had a number of outlying ranches which he visited regularly. He also spent a good deal of time with his neighbors, those who were big enough to be recognized. They were, Rose said bitterly, the aristocrats of the range.

On weekdays the family meals at the Bar D were eaten off the oilcloth-covered table in the kitchen. Dugan directed his conversation to Bonnie, he occasionally spoke to Rose, usually to complain about something she had or hadn't done, and he never said anything to Tommy.

It was the same with the Bar D foreman, Lew Roman, when Tommy happened to be with him around the corrals or barns. Roman, long-boned, bow-legged, and with a face dominated by a great beak of a nose, was Dugan's shadow in action and thought. Taking his cue from Dugan, Roman simply refused to recognize the fact that Tommy was alive.

Everyone else on the Bar D seemed to like Tommy from the first. The big vaquero, Pablo Garcia, talked to him an hour at a time, telling him about how it had been in California where a man didn't freeze his tail off as he did in this country.

Todd Moody, the youngest buckaroo on the ranch, initiated Tommy the first Sunday by getting him on Patches, a paint gelding that was the worst bucker on the place. Tommy won Todd's admiration by climbing back on for a second ride. The fact that Tommy was immediately thrown again didn't detract from Todd's respect.

There was Jim Becker, Dugan's partner on Mule Ear, a ranch to the west of the Bar D. He apparently had the same deal Bert Mayer had on the Lazy K. He showed up almost every Sunday afternoon because he lived alone, saying if he didn't have someone to talk to once a week, he'd get as loco as a sheep herder. He'd been in the Piute War a few years before and he told his experiences over and over to Tommy until Tommy could repeat them from memory.

That was the way it was with everyone down to Ole Crabbe and the Chinese cook, Ah Wing, Dugan and Roman the only exceptions. Tommy didn't understand it. When he mentioned it to Rose, she smiled.

"Lew Roman never has a thought he doesn't get from Mike," she said, "but it's different with the others. Maybe they're trying to make up for the way Mike acts, or maybe they just like you for what you are."

Tommy often thought about the evening when Dugan had agreed he could stay, and he said, "I guess Mike will always hate me."

Rose shook her head. "No, I don't think Mike really hates anyone. He doesn't love anyone, either. Oh, he thinks he loves Bonnie, but I don't think he does. Most of us need to love someone else. Maybe to hate, too, but Mike doesn't. He used to be different. He loved Bonnie's mother very much. She was young and beautiful, and he wanted to make a fortune for her. That was why he came here. After he started the Bar D, he brought her here, but she only lasted a year. She didn't see another woman for three months at a time. She left Mike and went back to California and got a divorce. Mike wouldn't let her have Bonnie. That's why I came."

She laid a hand on Tommy's shoulder. "I want you to stay here and I want you to be happy. Bonnie and I both need you. When you're older, you'll understand that better than you do now. Maybe someday Mike will change back to the way he used to be, but whether he does or not, we have to live the best we can. I want Bonnie to be able to love, Tommy. That's where you can help."

He nodded, only half understanding. He sensed from the first that Bonnie was fond of him. She often made a pest of herself, following him around like a puppy that was starved for affection.

Every morning from nine until noon Rose made Bonnie and Tommy stay in her little upstairs parlor that served as a schoolroom. She taught Bonnie reading, writing, arithmetic, and spelling, but she soon discovered there was little she could teach Tommy.

Bonnie was helped just to have Tommy around, Rose told him. She studied harder than she had, she showed more interest, and Rose finally admitted she'd been afraid Bonnie was stupid. Now she realized it had been nothing more serious than indifference.

All that Rose could do for Tommy was to encourage him to read. She had shelves of books in her parlor, many of them love stories Tommy refused to look at. But there were other kinds, too, histories and novels of adventure, and for the first time in his life, Tommy discovered James Fenimore Cooper.

Tommy found plenty of work to do outside, particularly on the woodpile. If the weather was good, Bonnie rode every afternoon. It was Tommy's job to saddle her bay mare Lady and a leggy sorrel that he called Cyclone, a name that always made Todd Moody laugh because he said Cyclone was about as much of a cyclone as Lady was.

On occasion Bonnie wanted a ride in her cart, and then Tommy harnessed her driving mare, a black named Julia. A heavy snow fell early in December, and then it was a sled instead of the cart. But whatever it was, Tommy spent part of each afternoon looking after Bonnie unless the weather was too bad to be outside.

The evenings were his own, and he could usually escape to his room with a book as soon as supper was eaten. This was partly to get away from Dugan when he was home. Too, Tommy liked to read, and it gave him an opportunity to get away from Bonnie for a few hours. Yet, he was not always successful, for sometimes when she couldn't sleep, she'd get out of bed and slip into his room wearing her nightgown, her blonde hair hanging down her back in long braids.

Bonnie would draw her chair up to the bed and ask, "Why do you like to read, Tommy?" Or she'd put her feet up on the bed beside his and say, "Look, my toes are shorter than yours." Or she'd sit looking at him as if deeply troubled, and then ask, "Tommy, why don't I have breasts like Aunt Rose?"

He never knew what she'd say or do, and she often embarrassed him and irritated him too by trespassing upon time that should have been his. But he couldn't bring himself to scold her or even to tell her she couldn't come in any more, for under no circumstances would he have knowingly hurt her feelings.

Every Sunday afternoon, if weather permitted, Tommy harnessed Rose's driving horse, hooked the animal up to the buggy, and watched Rose cross the creek and head northwest. He didn't know where she went, and if Bonnie knew, she didn't tell him. He had enough judgment to know he shouldn't ask since Rose hadn't volunteered to tell him.

Curiosity kept nagging him, especially when the weather turned cold in December, but still Rose took her Sunday drive, a wool cap pulled down around her ears, a buffalo robe over her lap, and her hands encased in fur-lined gloves. She usually returned after dark, Ole Crabbe putting her horse away, and she would come into the house with her cheeks cherry-red from the cold and immediately set to work getting supper, wearing her cloak of dignity just as she did through the week.

Three days before Christmas Rose sent Bonnie to her room to get ready for bed and asked Tommy to help her with the dishes. Dugan had been gone for a week and hadn't returned. As soon as Bonnie disappeared up the stairs, Rose said, "Bert wants you to spend Christmas with him and his family. Would you like to do that?"

He hadn't seen Mayer since the evening he had brought Tommy here to the Bar D. "Sure," Tommy said. "I'd like it a lot. I figured he'd forgotten all about me."

She shook her head gravely. "He'll never forget you." She washed another plate and dropped it into the pan holding the rinse water. "You'll like staying there. He has wonderful children. They don't have much in the way of presents, but they have a good time. We have presents, but we don't have a good time. The difference is that there's a great deal of love in the Mayer home, and very little on the Bar D."

Tommy dried a plate and put it down, thinking that she was right about there being little love on the Bar D. He remembered Mayer saying on their ride to the Bar D that no one would cry for Dugan if he died tomorrow, unless it was Bonnie.

Rose glanced at him, giving him a guarded smile. "Perhaps you're thinking Bonnie loves you and she loves me, and she thinks she loves her daddy, but he's a hard man to love. One of these days he'll do something to kill her love for him. Then he'll lose her the same way he lost her mother."

She took a long breath and was silent until she finished the dishes, then she said, "Maybe you don't know where I go on Sunday afternoons. Well, I go to see Bert. He wants me to marry him, but I promised Mike I'd stay with him until Bonnie's sixteen. Don't say anything about it to anyone. Please! And when you're at Bert's place, don't ask about the children's mother. She died a few days after the baby Arnie was born."

Rose took off her apron and hung it back of the stove. "You can leave in the morning and stay a week. You can ride Cyclone. Just follow the road you've seen me take and stay on it. You'll come to the Lazy K."

She paused, and then said with deep regret, "I wish I could send Bonnie, but I can't. I'd like for her to know what Christmas really is. You see, we lose the Christ child every year on the Bar D."

Tommy found the Lazy K on the high desert, the buildings set at the base of a fifty-foot rim, sagebrush and a few wind-shaped junipers around it. A small house with a lean-to for Mayer's daughter Cynthia, a slab barn and a few pole corrals, and furniture that was largely homemade.

He had not been in the house an hour when he knew what Rose had meant about the Mayer home. They made him welcome, Mayer shaking his hand, his melancholy face brightening with genuine pleasure; the girl Cynthia, who was fifteen and just beginning to be a woman, telling him how happy she was that he could come; the boy Pete, thirteen and as wind-burned and slim as his father, taking him out to the slab shed to see his colt; and the boy Arnie, redheaded and as active as a healthy pup, crawling up into his lap the instant he sat down.

On the morning of the day before Christmas, Mayer took Tommy and Pete on a long ride through the scattered junipers that dotted the high desert west of the Lazy K, returning near noon with a tree that was so perfectly shaped that Cynthia cried out with delight when she saw it.

Tommy and Pete made a stand for it and Cynthia placed it in the corner of the room. They spent the afternoon decorating it with strings of tinsel that had been saved for years, chains made of rings of colored paper, strings of pop corn, and a few bright geegaws cut from a shiny tin can.

After supper on Christmas Eve, Mayer read the Christmas story from Luke. They sang several carols, then had their presents, inexpensive things and nothing like the presents Tommy had received when his folks had been alive, but they were presents and it was Christmas, and no one measured the worth of a gift by the money it cost.

Tommy, sitting in a corner with his gifts on his lap, a bright neckerchief and a pair of socks, discovered a lump in his throat that he couldn't swallow. In this moment he was a small boy again, a sharp and poignant memory of his past Christmases brought back into his mind, and of his home and parents that had been taken from him.

He found it hard to leave when the week was over. Mayer and Pete shook hands with him, and Cynthia shyly told him he would be welcome any time he could visit them. As he mounted even little Arnie waved at him.

When he had ridden to the Lazy K, Tommy had passed a small stone house. On his way back he stopped and went inside. It was here, Mayer had said, that he visited with Rose on Sundays. The distance to the Lazy K was too far for her to travel in an afternoon, so it was more convenient to meet at this halfway place than for her to go all the way to Mayer's home.

The stone house had belonged to a settler who had been driven out of the country years ago by Dugan. There was nothing in it now but two chairs and a table. The fireplace had fresh ashes, but even with a fire it seemed to Tommy that the room would be a cold place in which to spend a Sunday afternoon this time of year.

As Tommy rode on toward the Bar D, he remembered Mayer's cautioning words, "Don't let her start out if it looks like a storm's coming. She's not afraid of anything, and she knows how much I want to see her, but I can't let anything happen to her." He laid a hand on Tommy's shoulder. "Help me take care of her. That's why I wanted you there. She needs someone."

It was true. Rose needed Bert Mayer and Mayer certainly needed her. He had told Tommy about his wife, how she had wandered away into the desert a few days after Arnie was born and got lost. A storm had come up and they hadn't found her body for three days.

"She must have gone kind of crazy," Mayer had said. "The loneliness and all. She kept wanting me to break up with Dugan and move, but I wouldn't do it."

He blamed himself. He didn't say so, but Tommy knew it was true, and he couldn't keep from asking, "Why don't you break up with him? Ben Lampe said you hated him."

"Lampe was right," Mayer said. "I guess almost everybody hates Mike Dugan. Even Rose."

Then he was silent for a long time, his big-knuckled hands laced in front of him, cradling his chin. Finally he said, "I didn't have anything until Dugan set me up here on this spread. He's got several other outfits like this one all around the Bar D, sort of outposts that protect the heart of his empire. It's good sense, too, because we all work harder than we would just drawing wages. I make more money this way than I could at anything else, and I don't like to pull out when I'm doing so well. Hating Dugan's got nothing to do with it. He's not hard to get along with. Fact is, I don't see him very often. He leaves almost everything to me." He paused, then added bitterly, "Almost everything."

He shook his head and rose. "That's not the real reason I stay, Tommy. I tell myself it is, but I know different. The truth is I keep remembering what the Bible says about a man reaping what he sows. Mike Dugan's got a hell of a crop to gather, and I want to be here when he does his harvesting."

Now, as the cold night settled down around him, Tommy stared ahead at the lights in the Bar D buildings, and he wondered if he would be here to see Mike Dugan harvest his crop. He thought about Dugan, strong and capable and ambitious, a man who shaped events and people to advance his interests. Nothing could change him except Bonnie's tears.

Tommy splashed across the creek with its lacy fringe of ice. He would stay the winter, he thought. He owed that to Bert Mayer and to Rose. He didn't have to. He knew Mayer would give him a place to stay, but he had a debt to pay and he would pay it.

But what would he do come spring? He didn't know. He just didn't know.

BOOK II   THE YOUTH

chapter 8

STARBUCK WAS A NEW TOWN sprawled in the sagebrush, a year-old infant. Like Minerva from the brain of Jove, it had sprung full grown from the mind of Mike Dugan. It was more than an investment; it was a weapon by which he hoped to defeat the settlers. Very likely he could, too, for he had set up the machinery by which he could control credit and transportation, the twin arteries that gave life blood to any rural community.

Dugan had tried to get the other big ranchers in the area to back him, particularly Sam Bell, who owned Arrow on the east side of Two Medicine Peaks, and Marvin Gentry, whose Wineglass occupied most of Indian Valley which lay north of Dugan's Bar D. But they said they had enough to do without bucking the "plow pushers" who were beginning to move into the country in considerable numbers, so Dugan went ahead on his own, building his town on Duck River near the foothills of the Blue Mountains in Indian Valley, a good twenty miles north of the Bar D.

Dugan started a store because the people who were settling in Indian Valley needed one, and he brought in a man named Sylvester Chase to operate it. He established the Starbuck State Bank because the people needed that too, and picked Russ Ordway to run it for him. The people needed local government, so he pulled all the political wires he could and Starbuck County was created, Dugan seeing to it that a man of his choice, Broncho Quinn, was the sheriff. To complete his hold on the county, he organized stage and freight lines that connected Starbuck with Canyon City to the north.

Tommy Gordon had seen all this happen in the five years since he had ridden north with Bert Mayer. He didn't question any of it. Having worked for Mike Dugan first as a chore boy and Bonnie's companion, then as a buckaroo, he had learned that Mike Dugan demanded one basic response from all his employees: an intangible he called loyalty.

Loyalty, as Todd Moody said, was like a strip of rubber. It stretched to include almost everything. Doing a day's work, for one thing, and more during roundup. Having a man's guts when it came to a fight. And above everything else, obeying Dugan's orders without question. Here was where the shoe pinched for Tommy; he obeyed or he lost his job, and sometimes it was not an easy decision.

Now, on a hot Saturday in late July, he stood at the bar in the Red Bull Saloon in Starbuck nursing a drink he didn't want. Dugan and the Bar D crew were there, some at the bar and others sitting at poker tables. Most of the townsmen, too, for Saturday afternoons gave them an opportunity to listen to Dugan and get their orders. Not that he gave them as orders, but the businessmen knew that was what they were. Watching

67

Dugan, who sat at a poker table with Chase and Ordway, Tommy was reminded that these five years had brought no change to Dugan except to accentuate the characteristics which he'd had as long as Tommy had known him.

But Tommy had changed. He stood as tall as Dugan, slender and long-boned, giving a sort of sprouting-up appearance as if he'd shot up from his boots overnight. He could handle himself; he had learned the skills of his trade, thanks to Todd Moody, who was his friend. On the Bar D you learned or you got fired, and Tommy was quick to learn.

Dugan seemed to have been bypassed by time. He hadn't taken on a pound of weight; his hair and sweeping mustache were as red as ever. He still had the aggressive air of a man who pushes everything aside that's in the way, just as he had pushed Tommy aside that day at the shipping pens in Winnemucca. If anything, he was more arrogant and aggressive than ever.

Eddie Vance drifted in from the street. Seeing Tommy at the bar, he walked to him. Vance published the *Starbuck Weekly Herald* and was the one man in Starbuck who didn't belong to Mike Dugan. How long that situation would last was a question in Tommy's mind.

"Howdy, Tommy," Vance said. "Drinking alone?"

Tommy shook his head. "Todd Moody hasn't got here yet, so I've been watching the king and his court."

Vance grinned as the bartender poured his drink. When the barman moved away, Vance said, "Hooray for the revolution." He nodded at the filled glass beside Tommy's elbow. "You're not much business, son."

"No, guess not," Tommy said.

Vance jerked his head at Lew Roman, who was standing at the far end of the bar. "Now there's a drinking man for you."

Tommy glanced at Roman. The foreman had been working steadily at the project of getting drunk from the moment he'd come through the bat wings. He drank himself into insensibility nearly every Saturday afternoon. By evening some of the Bar D hands would carry him into the back room where he'd sleep it off.

"You know," Tommy said, "when I first signed on, Lew didn't drink much. Not like this."

"You know why he's drinking now?"

"No."

"It's simple," Vance said. "He's got to forget. Old ambitions. Old dreams. The right to call himself a man." Vance put a hand on Tommy's shoulder. "Get off the Bar D before it happens to you."

Tommy looked at him in surprise. "What are you talking about?"

"Mike Dugan. He consumes everyone around him. It'll happen to your friend Todd. Maybe it already has." He withdrew his hand as he tipped his head in a short nod at the table where Dugan sat with Ordway and Chase. "Look at them, boy. They're sucking

69

Dugan's milk. That's what turns them into machines serving Mike Dugan."

Tommy watched Ordway and Chase for a moment, both leaning forward to listen to what Dugan was saying. He shook his head, his gaze returning to Vance. "You make it too simple, Eddie."

"In Indian Valley and on the Frying Pan you're a free man or you belong to Dugan," Vance said. "What could be simpler?"

"What about you?"

"I'm a free man," Vance said indignantly. "Ever know me to be anything else?"

"Not yet."

"What do you mean by that?"

"There'll come a day," Tommy said. "You know that as well as I do."

"What kind of a day?"

"The bank's loaning money to farmers, isn't it?" Tommy asked. "They get here with a little money, but it's soon gone, and the way things are, they won't have a cash crop for a while. In the end they'll lose their shirts to Mike. What will you do then? Ignore it?"

Vance lifted his glass, gulped his drink, and shuddered. "They call this a lubricating parlor, but the stuff they sell don't lubricate. It just eats your insides out."

"Well, will you?"

Vance placed his ink-stained hands on the bar and stared at them. He said, "I won't ignore it."

"Then you'll get hell beaten out of you."

"You know what the big man is," Vance said bitterly. "Why do you keep on working for him?"

"I don't know," Tommy said. "I don't even know if I'm honest enough to find the answer."

The hammer of hoofs in the streets turned Tommy's attention to the door. A moment later Todd Moody charged through the bat wings and strode directly to Dugan's table. He said something and Dugan nodded and rose. He glanced at Roman, saw that he was well on the way to being drunk, then let his gaze sweep the room, bringing it to bear on Tommy.

Dugan hesitated, his face speculative, then he said curtly, "Gordon," and strode out of the saloon, Moody following.

"There'll come a day for you, too," Vance said softly. "Maybe this is it."

"Maybe," Tommy said, and left the saloon, his drink still on the bar.

Vance looked at the glass of whisky, then picked it up and drank it. "Varnish," he said.

He wiped his mouth on his sleeve and walked out, a troubled man.

chapter 9

TOMMY FELT A TRANSIENT QUALITY about Starbuck every time he was in town, always wondering if it would be here in another five years. There were no sidewalks, and when it rained, which was seldom, Main Street became loblolly.

No lawns, no trees, not even a bush or a flower garden. Sagebrush surrounded the town, but it had been grubbed out of Main Street. The half-dozen false-fronted business buildings and the frame dwellings did not form any kind of pattern. All of them faced Main Street, came crowding the hitch rails, some set back twenty feet or more.

It always struck Tommy that nothing in Starbuck showed the careful planning that had gone into the arrangement of the Bar D buildings. Mike Dugan might as well have said that the town was second-class, cheaply and carelessly built, but good enough for the farmers.

Tommy untied his horse, and mounting, followed Dugan and Todd Moody out of town, riding south. Several teams and wagons stood in front of the store and Finley's Bar. A farm woman came out of the store with an armload of bundles. Her husband lurched through the door of Finley's Bar, and she turned on him, scolding him in a shrewish voice. Children were playing in the street, most of them with dirty faces and runny noses, their clothes consisted largely of patches sewed upon patches.

Dugan didn't speak to the farmer or his wife. He ignored the settlers as he ignored everything he didn't like, never doubting that the course of events which would be shaped by his planning would take care of these people and they would soon be gone.

Dugan didn't say anything until he had ridden a quarter of a mile, then he burst out, "By God, how can they be crazy enough to think they can make a living in a cattle country?"

"Don't ask me," Todd said. "I don't savvy it either."

After that they rode in silence, holding a little to the east of south. The road paralleled Duck River, which lay to the west. It took a meandering course across the north half of the valley to spread out through the tules and cattails that surrounded Indian Lake.

Behind the men the foothills held a few runty junipers, and on beyond the lower slopes were the long, high ridges of the Blue Mountains which were covered by fir and pine. The settlers had made their homes in the foothills wherever they could find a stream that broke out of the mountains. Here there was ample game, timber to build cabins, wood for fuel, and protection, they thought, against the cruel winter winds.

But the future of the valley lay south toward the lakes where the sage gave way to grass. Marvin Gentry had known this, and so had settled a mile north of the swamp, building between the road and Duck River, but his ranch had not been developed, largely because he lacked the ruthless drive that characterized Dugan. It was only a question of time until Gentry would have to sell and Wineglass would drop like a rich plum into the waiting hand of Mike Dugan.

Dugan made no secret of his ambition. He had offered what he considered a fair price, and Gentry had turned him down. Now, as Dugan came opposite the Wineglass buildings, he gestured toward them,

73

saying, "Ordway just told me that Gentry came in the first of the week and borrowed $5,000. I'll give him till spring."

Todd Moody laughed. "I always figured Marvin for more sense than that. He'll lose a chunk of money by not taking the offer you made last June."

"Sure he will," Dugan said. "He'll walk out with nothing."

The road swung east around Indian Lake, and again they rode in silence. Tommy stared at Dugan's broad back that seemed to strain against the seams of his coat, and pondered Eddie Vance's words: "Get off the Bar D before it happens to you." Eddie had asked him why he stayed and he had failed to give the proper answer. He knew, all right. It was Bonnie Dugan, a woman at sixteen and one who would marry him tomorrow if she could.

Bonnie had been fond of him from the day he had first come to the Bar D. He would never forget how Dugan had blown up when he'd found Tommy in his house and how Bonnie had dropped the doll Dugan had brought and cried as if her heart were broken because she wanted Tommy to stay. Nothing Rose had said had influenced Dugan, but Bonnie's tears had.

So Tommy had stayed, hated by Dugan and therefore ignored by him. Dugan would have liked nothing better than for Tommy to draw his time and ride off, but because of Bonnie, he couldn't, or wouldn't, fire Tommy.

When Tommy was seventeen, Dugan sent him to

74

work for Bert Mayer on the Lazy K. The following summer he rode for Jim Becker on Mule Ear. After that he stayed at the Bar D, but he didn't move back into the house. He was part of the crew the same as Todd Moody and the rest, still disliked by Lew Roman and so given the dirty end of the stick time after time.

Tommy often wondered what had happened to Ben Lampe and Dora Lind, but Dugan never let Tommy go south with the trail herd to Winnemucca, intimating that Tommy wasn't a good enough hand. Bert Mayer told Tommy that Lampe and Dora had left Winnemucca, but he didn't know where they had gone, or even if they had left together.

Tommy had no way of finding out what had driven Lampe and Dora from Winnemucca, but he felt Dugan was to blame. It was something else he would have to settle for, one small thing added to many.

The thought occurred to Tommy that the greatest punishment he could give Dugan would be to run off with Bonnie. But he couldn't. Rose had done a fine job raising Bonnie, effectively resisting Dugan's efforts to spoil her. She was too good to be used as a weapon against her father. Besides, Tommy was in love with her, a discovery that startled him, for he had been slow to realize that she was far from the child he had been hired to look after.

Tommy was surprised when Dugan and Todd swung west just south of Indian Lake and rode along the fence that Dugan had built to mark the north edge of the Bar D range. It ran from the westernmost point of the Two Medicine Peaks range past the tip of the swamp that lay south of the lakes and on across the Frying Pan to the rimrock that formed the eastern edge of the desert.

The fence was on government land; therefore Dugan had no right to build it, a fact that didn't bother him in the slightest. He said blandly that it prevented Bar D cattle from drifting north, but the real purpose was to keep settlers out of the Frying Pan valley, and Dugan would have admitted it if he had been pressed.

From the time they had left Starbuck, Dugan had given no hint why they were here or why he had brought Tommy. He didn't say anything even after they turned north along the western edge of the swamp and came to a cabin built by a man named Corrigan who had settled here early in the summer with a wife and small boy, but now Tommy had no need for explanations.

Apparently Corrigan had seen them coming, for he stood in front of the cabin waiting. Neither his wife nor boy was in sight. Corrigan wasn't armed, but he was a big man, acting as if he were confident he could take care of himself.

As Dugan stepped down, Corrigan said, "I already told your man I wasn't leaving."

Dugan started toward him in slow, deliberate steps. Corrigan, nervous, said hurriedly, "This has been officially declared swamp land. I bought a full section from the state and paid for it. I'm north of your fence, so you've got no call to come bothering me."

Still Dugan moved toward him, not hesitating and not saying a word. Corrigan shouted at him, "You're trespassing on my land. Get off."

Dugan was only a step from Corrigan. Suddenly he exploded, a big fist cracking Corrigan squarely on the jaw and knocking him flat. A woman screamed from the doorway, "Let him alone or I'll kill you."

She held a shotgun lined on Dugan's back. Todd had his pistol in his hand. He said coldly, "Drop it, ma'am, or I'll plug your husband."

She turned her head to stare at him, her mouth springing open, her face ghastly white. She laid the shotgun on the ground, then straightened up, an arm going around the boy who had run out of the cabin to stand beside her.

Dugan didn't even bother to waste a glance on the woman. Corrigan had been dazed by the blow. He sat up, head tipped back to look at Dugan.

"You were warned to move on," Dugan said. "Yesterday was your last day."

He kicked Corrigan on the side of the head and Corrigan fell flat on his back. Dugan kicked him three times in the side, hard, brutal kicks delivered with all the power in his massive legs. Corrigan's ribs must have been broken. The woman screamed invectives, but she stayed where she was, her arm around the shrieking boy. Corrigan was unconscious, or nearly so.

Dugan swung around to face the woman. "Get out. If you're still here tomorrow noon, I'll kill your husband and burn your shack."

He mounted and rode back the way he had come, Todd Moody still holding his pistol on the woman. She was screaming, "I'll have you arrested, you murdering son of a bitch." Dugan kept on riding, not looking around. Todd holstered his pistol, and rode after Dugan.

Tommy followed, sick at the stomach. He had sat his saddle and watched it, as cruel a thing as he had ever seen in his life. He should have done something, but he hadn't, and he would be ashamed as long as he lived.

He wondered why Dugan had brought him. He had no answer, but he knew Dugan had a reason. Mike Dugan never did anything without a reason.

chapter 10

THE BAR D was the most impressive-appearing ranch Tommy had ever seen. The physical setting helped, for Mike Dugan had chosen his ranch site with the same shrewdness that marked all of his ventures. North Medicine Peak lifted its great bulk to the east in a series of ridges, its crest retaining a cape of snow well into the summer. On the west the rimrock rose two or three hundred feet directly above the level valley of the Frying Pan, and from here gave the appearance of being a gigantic ruler laid against the sky.

Between North Medicine Peak and the rimrock, Frying Pan Creek rolled northward to Indian Lake.

78

Originally a willow jungle had covered both sides of the creek just as it did Duck River south of Starbuck, but except for a narrow line of brush on both banks, the willows had been grubbed out long ago.

Hay meadows ran from the south tip of the swamp that surrounded Indian Lake on up the creek nearly to its head. Stacks of hay dotted the meadows, some carried over from the previous summer. In the fifteen years Mike Dugan had been here, he had never suffered any serious winter loss, for he always saw to it that he had hay to spare.

But the buildings themselves impressed Tommy more than the physical background, for it was here that Dugan demonstrated his ability to plan. When he first came, he had planted a row of Lombardy poplars in front of the house and had put a fence around them so that stock couldn't get at them. Now the trees made a tall line of green that threw a solid bank of shade in the hot summer afternoons across the grassy front yard. The two-story frame house always looked bright and fresh, receiving a coat of white paint every three years.

Upstream on a bench above the road Dugan had scraped out a racetrack, banking it gently so that it drained well. Beside the track was a stable for his racehorses and a small house for a man whose sole duty was to care for these horses. Races were held nearly every Sunday during the summer, but the gala occasion was on the Fourth of July when people flocked in from fifty miles around, even the farmers from the north edge of Indian Valley making the trip to the Bar D.

There were races in the morning and the afternoon of the Fourth with as much as $20,000 being bet, the bulk of it winding up in Mike Dugan's pocket, but he played the genial host so well that no one kicked. As Sam Bell put it ruefully, "It's a pleasure to lose to Mike Dugan."

The ranch house faced the creek. Behind it were outhouses, the woodshed, and the meat house. The rest of the buildings were some distance upstream and across the road: bunk-house, cook shack, a huge, sprawling barn, and some sheds and smaller buildings, along with the stockade corrals which were made by placing juniper posts close together in a trench and lashing willows into place on top with rawhide.

Riding in from the north as Tommy was now, it always struck him that the Bar D was more of a town than Starbuck. Dugan had spent fifteen years creating the Bar D. No one, not even Rose or Bonnie, had any idea how wealthy Dugan was. He was thirty-seven, a man at the height of his powers. Tommy often wondered where his ambition would take him, what he would do and where he would be in another fifteen years.

There must be a limit to the size to which a man could grow, Tommy thought, as he turned off the road toward the corrals. Dugan had already dismounted and was waiting for him, his face wiped clean of expression.

Todd, too, was on his feet, his gaze on Dugan.

Tommy stepped down, and as he made a half turn to face Dugan, the big man moved forward and slapped Tommy across the right cheek, a hard blow that swiveled his head partly around and almost knocked him down.

It happened so fast and unexpectedly that Tommy had no defense. He was jarred and hurt and a little dazed, Dugan and Todd and the horse whirling uncertainly in front of him. Dugan's brittle words reached him, "If you're going to be a Bar D man, Gordon, you'll act like one."

He turned on his heel and strode across the road and through the poplars and on into the house. He hadn't gone ten feet when Tommy recovered from shock, and a crazy, consuming fury possessed him. He reached for his gun, for the first time since he had been here really wanting to kill Mike Dugan.

"Better not, Tommy," Todd Moody said.

Tommy turned his head. Moody's gun was on him. Tommy's hand dropped away from his pistol. He said, "I wasn't going to shoot him in the back. I guess he could draw faster'n me and he'd kill me, but by God, Todd, you don't expect me to let that go?"

"That's exactly what I expect," Todd said. "He'd kill you all right, and I don't want that to happen. I kind of like you, although sometimes I wonder why."

Tommy rubbed the side of his face where Dugan had struck him. He demanded, "What did he do it for?"

"Because you sat on your horse like a damned bump while he worked on Corrigan," Todd said. "He's told

81

me more'n once you didn't fit Bar D's style. I told him you did, that you just needed a chance. Well, he gave it to you and you proved him right."

"What'd he expect me to do?" Tommy demanded. "Get down and help kick Corrigan to death?"

"No, but there was a woman with a shotgun and a kid. I could keep the woman covered, but after she dropped the shotgun, even the kid could have picked it up and blowed Mike's head off."

"He was just a baby. You think I'd have shot him?"

"A baby can pull a trigger," Todd said. "You'd better have shot him if it meant saving Mike's life. And another thing. Corrigan might have had a hideout on him. He could have pulled it on Mike."

"Half knocked out and lying on the ground?" Tommy demanded.

"Mike ain't one to gamble with his life," Todd said. "Neither would I if I had the world by the tail and a downhill pull like he's got. He needed two guns to make sure. That's why he fetched you along. Well, he wound up with one and he didn't like it."

Tommy stared at Todd rebelliously, not realizing until this moment how completely Todd Moody belonged to Mike Dugan. Todd was older than he was, but he never thought of him that way. To Tommy, Todd was the same freckle-faced kid, brash and hard-riding, that he had met in Winnemucca and who had put him on a bad horse the first Sunday he'd been on the Bar D and slapped him on the back when he got back on after taking a bad spill.

Tommy knew now he couldn't have been more wrong. It struck him that Todd had a tough, predatory look about him. He might have been a young Lew Roman. Maybe he was being groomed to take Roman's place. Tommy remembered Eddie Vance saying that Dugan consumed everyone around him and it would happen to Todd, that maybe it had already. Vance had been right.

Tommy gave his back to Todd, and removing saddle and bridle from his horse, turned him into the pasture. He walked to the bunkhouse and lay down on his bunk. The fire of fury had burned down to smoldering coals, enabling him to think coherently. He hated Dugan enough to kill him and he had reason to do it, but Todd was right. If he jumped Dugan, Dugan would kill him. There was no profit in that.

He was done on the Bar D. He wasn't worried about the future the way he had been when he'd stepped off the train at Winnemucca with nine dollars in his pocket. He owned a roan gelding named Slats, he owned his saddle, and he had a little better than $200 saved. He'd do all right until he found a job.

He might spend the winter with Bert Mayer. He'd be welcome, and there was always enough work to do around the Lazy K to earn his keep. He might even go back to Prairie City and look up his Aunt Sadie. He'd given a good deal of thought to that lately. She had taken advantage of him and robbed him. If he gave her fat neck a twist, she'd settle up with him.

Then he thought of Bonnie. She wouldn't want him

to leave and he didn't want to leave her. But there wasn't anything else he could do. He had to go.

He ate supper that night in the cook shack with Todd. Both were silent, Todd uneasy now that he was alone with Tommy and had had time to think about what had happened, and Tommy not giving a damn one way or the other. The old relationship with Todd was gone and it would never come back.

After he finished eating, Tommy walked slowly to the corral. The sun was hanging just above the rim-rock, the place strangely quiet with the crew in town.

He thought again of the Corrigans. The shame of having done nothing when Dugan was kicking Corrigan rose in him once more and became almost unbearable. Finally, because he could not stand doing nothing and because he had to know about Corrigan, he saddled Slats and took the road down the creek, crossed it, and swung around the southern tip of the swamp.

No lights showed in the Corrigan cabin as he rode up. He wondered about it, for it was dusk now, the cabin and slab shed dark shapes in front of him. He called out, but there was no answer. Dismounting, he went into the cabin. The door wasn't latched and was banging in the wind.

He struck a match. The cabin had been cleaned out, hastily, he judged, from the mess that littered the floor. He went outside, closing the door behind him. He expected the Corrigans to leave, but not today after the beating the man had taken.

For a time Tommy stood there, staring across the valley at the rimrock with the last color fading from the sky above it. He thought of the rank injustice of this, of the dreams the Corrigans must have had, probably putting all their money into this section of land, most of it not being swamp land at all, not more than fifty acres next to the lake which could be drained and turned into fine hay land.

That was the way with much of this country. Thousands of acres had been turned over to the state as swamp land without being properly investigated. The state in turn had sold it to cowmen like Dugan and Gentry, and smaller bits to settlers like Corrigan. The right and wrong of it didn't matter. What did matter was that Corrigan had every right to his section, legally and morally, and Dugan had none. From a practical standpoint that didn't matter either, the law in this country being what it was. But it mattered to Tommy.

He mounted and rode back to the Bar D, wishing he could live over just a few minutes of the afternoon while he had sat his saddle and watched Mike Dugan smash Corrigan's body with one brutal kick after another.

chapter 11

TOMMY DID NOT ATTEMPT TO SEE BONNIE Sunday morning. Dugan remained home, working on his books and then drifting down to the racetrack to watch his horses exercise. Most of the crew followed, giving Tommy a chance to pack his warsack and check over his gear without being questioned.

Another surprising thing, now that he had reached the actual breaking point and could look back over these years, was the fact that he had no close friends among the Bar D crew. Lew Roman frankly disliked him. The rest were friendly enough, but being friendly was a long ways from being friends. What Todd Moody had said and done yesterday was harsh proof of this very point.

Tommy sat down on his bunk and smoked a cigarette, going over this in his mind. Who had been his friends since his folks had died, the people who had shaped his life and given it direction? Certainly Ben Lampe and Dora Lind.

After he'd come to the Bar D, he'd name Rose Dugan. Bert Mayer, of course. Bert's son Pete. Cynthia, Bert's daughter, who was still home and unmarried, looking out for Bert and Pete and her young brother Arnie. In town? No one but Eddie Vance.

After dinner Dugan and Todd rode north, probably to see if Corrigan had left. Tommy saddled his chestnut, lashed his warsack behind the saddle, and leaving his gelding tied in front of the house, went in. He hadn't been here for a long time, Dugan having made it clear that he belonged in the bunkhouse with the rest of the crew.

Tommy seldom saw Bonnie except on occasions such as this when Dugan was gone. Not that they had been given specific orders they couldn't see each other. It was simply easier not to slap Dugan in the face, feeling the way they did about each other.

Rose was finishing the dishes in the kitchen when Tommy came in. She smiled over her shoulder at him and asked, "Want a piece of pie? It's custard that Bonnie baked this morning."

Tommy shook his head. "No thanks. I just wanted to see Bonnie for a minute."

Rose laughed. "This will come as no surprise to you, but she was expecting you. She's upstairs putting on her riding clothes now."

"I can't stay long enough to take a ride," Tommy said. "I'm leaving. I just wanted to tell Bonnie goodby."

Rose didn't say anything for a moment, but she was visibly shaken. She dried the last dish, then hung the dish cloth behind the stove to dry and went to him. She had aged in these five years, aged far more than she should have. She was still a graceful, attractive woman, retaining the dignity Tommy had noticed the first time he had seen her, but there were touches of gray in her auburn hair and her eyes were surrounded by a fine network of lines.

You either fought Mike Dugan or you surrendered, and Rose never surrendered. She would have an easier life if she did, Tommy thought. As long as she resisted, she was under tremendous pressure. She was a rock and Dugan was a ceaseless wind, constantly probing for soft spots and eroding them. In the end he would destroy her if she stayed. Her only hope was to marry Bert Mayer, and Tommy wasn't sure that Bert was strong enough to take care of her.

She put her hands on Tommy's shoulders and looked up at him, silent for a moment while her eyes searched his face. Then she asked, "Did Mike fire you?"

"No, but he would have a long time ago if it hadn't been for you and Bonnie."

"Then you've got to stay, for Bonnie's sake," Rose said. "You don't see each other as often as you'd like, and maybe you're too young to get married, but you do a lot for her just by being here."

He shook his head. "I can't stay, Rose. Not even for Bonnie."

"If you knew how often she stands by the window just to get a glimpse of you when you ride out with the crew." Rose's lips trembled as she turned away from him. "What will you tell her?"

"I don't know."

Rose sat down at the table. "There's no use trying to explain Mike or even understand him. We've got to accept him as he is. Bonnie is his weakness. In one way he's spoiled her, but in another he's made her into his image. You're the only link she has with being a whole person. If you go, I don't know what will happen to her."

He didn't know what Rose meant about Bonnie "being a whole person." He did know that any right to call himself a man would be lost if he stayed.

"I've got to go," he said.

He was aware of the misery that was in her, of the worry, of the pulling and hauling between what she wanted to do and her reluctance to go against her brother's wishes. Dugan needed her to keep house for him, and he would hold her as long as he could.

"Rose, you've got to leave here," he burst out. "Marry Bert, or Mike will keep you here all your life."

"I'm going to leave," she said dully, "but I can't yet."

He would have pressed it, but Bonnie came in then, wearing a tan riding skirt and a green blouse, a bright orange scarf around her neck. Her blond hair was brushed back from her forehead and pinned in a bun on the back of her head. She was more than a pretty girl; she was exciting and vital, and every time Tommy looked at her he wondered how she could possibly be the chubby child who used to come into his room when he wanted to read and ask why she didn't have breasts like Aunt Rose. She had them now, firm breasts that pressed sharply against her blouse, and trim hips and thighs that made provocative curves under her skirt. She was as much of a woman at sixteen as Cynthia Mayer was at eighteen.

She was boisterous at times, and she was now, letting out a whoop when she saw him. She ran to him, saying gaily, "It's time you showed up." She kissed him, her hands caressing his cheeks, and asked, "When are you going to marry me?"

"I don't know."

"I'm a hussy or I wouldn't be asking you," she said, "but you keep putting me off. I'm not going to wait forever."

"I know that," he said. "I don't expect you to."

"I've got an old dragon for a father," she said. "You've just got to beard him in his den the way Sir Lancelot would have done. Aunt Rose can handle him if you can't."

"No," Rose said sharply. "I can't."

Bonnie turned to Rose, shocked by her aunt's tone, and then swung back to Tommy. "What's wrong? Tommy, you look like you're sick."

"He is," Rose said. "So am I. He's leaving the Bar D." Bonnie shrank back as if he had struck her. She whispered, "You're joking."

"No," Tommy said. "I'm leaving. I'm not even going to ask your dad for what's coming to me. I'm riding out. If it hadn't been for you, I'd have done it before."

"I'm still here," she said. "I still love you. Nothing's changed." She bit her lip, her eyes questioning him. "Maybe you don't love me any more."

"Nothing's changed that way," he said. "I am sick, from loving you and not wanting to leave you, but I've got to."

"Why?" she cried. "Just give me one reason why."

"Your dad," he said.

"This is crazy, Tommy. We can go on just like we have. I know he'd blow up if we told him we were getting married, but sooner or later we've got to. We'll do it tonight and just let him blow up."

"No, don't do it," Rose said. "You don't know your father very well. Not the way I do. He'd let you have your way in most things, but on something like this, he'd go crazy. I don't know what he'd do. Maybe send you away."

"I won't go," she said, her lips firming out. "I just won't go." She stepped close to Tommy, her hands on his. "What's happened that made you talk like this?"

He hesitated, glancing at Rose, who nodded. "You haven't told me, either."

He told them about the beating Corrigan had received, and about Dugan slapping him when they reached the Bar D and what Todd had said. "I just sat there and watched Corrigan get a beating that may kill him. After your dad cracked me one, I think I would have killed him if Todd hadn't stopped me. Or tried to. If anybody else had hit me, Todd or Lew or Pablo, or any of them, I'd have fought them. But that's the trouble. Nobody fights Mike."

"And lives," Rose added.

"I guess I'd feel the same if I were in your place, Tommy," Bonnie said as she turned toward the dining-room door. "Let's take a ride together. The last one. Then I'll let you go."

91

He hesitated, glancing at Rose, but she had turned her head to stare out of the window and so gave him no help.

Bonnie had stopped in the doorway and was looking back at him over her shoulder, smiling in a way that told him how much she wanted him to come. It was wrong, he told himself. Better just ride off and make a clean break.

"Come on," she said. "I'm only asking for an hour. Maybe two. Is that too much to give me?"

"No," he said. "I'll saddle your mare."

chapter 12

WITHOUT A WORD being spoken between them, Bonnie and Tommy swung around the house and struck off up the slope of North Medicine Peak. It was as if each knew the other wanted to go to Twin Springs, which was well up on a shoulder of the mountain. They reached it in half an hour, Bonnie's favorite spot where she had made Tommy take her so often when she'd been a child.

Here were trees, grass and shade, with two small streams seeping out of the ground even in late August. Bonnie stepped down and threw herself on the grass, stretching and yawning. Tommy loosened the cinches and left the reins dragging, thinking they would not be here long.

He sat down beside her as she reached out for his hand. He remembered how he used to resign himself to coming here while Bonnie fired questions at him so fast he didn't have time to answer. Looking back on that first year when he had been with her every day, he thought that he had actually disliked her because she was such a pest. Now he knew he hadn't.

Thinking about it, he realized there had been a strange and wonderful intimacy between them. To him she had been the little sister he'd never had, and to her he was the big brother who was capable of handling any emergency.

He'd never had to prove his courage or strength to her. She read Rose's books about the Greek myths, the ancient, gory fairy tales, and the stories of King Arthur and his knights. She had been convinced that if he had lived in any of those times, he would have been Hercules or Prince Charming or Sir Lancelot.

He rolled a smoke and struck a match and held the flame to the cigarette, trying not to think of those days when she had trusted him implicitly and he had reveled in that trust even though he had not been aware of it.

Or when she had come into his room without either Rose or her father knowing and had insisted on talking when he wanted to read, or had crawled into bed with him because she was cold, she said, and he could get her warm. That had made him uneasy more than anything else she had ever done, and he'd tried to make her go back to her own room, but she'd refuse, snuggling closer to him and shivering. There had been nothing he could do except call Rose, and he had been unwilling to do that.

She jarred his thoughts by asking, "What are you going to do, Tommy? Where are you going to go?"

"I don't know," he said. "I'll go see Bert first. I'll decide then."

"You be careful," she said angrily. "Cynthia's in love with you. She always has been."

He looked at her in amazement. "That's the craziest thing I ever heard."

"You like her, don't you?"

"Sure, she's all right. I like Pete and Arnie, too."

"But she's not pretty, is she?" Bonnie pressed. "She's awful plain."

She was, but he didn't want to agree with Bonnie. "Oh, I don't know. She's got pretty eyes."

"You make me so mad." She reached up and pulled him down beside her. "I don't want to quarrel if this is to be our last Sunday together. I don't want to get mad at you, either, but I will if you don't kiss me."

He kissed her, and then he had to pull away from her and sit up. There was a hunger in her lips, a demanding, passionate desire he had never sensed before, and suddenly he was frightened. Maybe the hunger was in him, not Bonnie; maybe he couldn't handle himself, and he didn't want to do anything to spoil this last hour.

She moved and laid her head on his lap, smiling up at him, mischief lurking in the corners of her mouth as it used to when she was planning some crazy, tomboy prank. "You thinking about me? Or Cynthia?"

"Will you forget Cynthia?" he said angrily.

Her smile disappeared. "Well, what were you thinking about?"

"Just looking at the scenery," he said. "I guess this is the prettiest place I ever saw."

The ranch buildings below them looked like toys. He could see a great distance up and down the Frying Pan, with the new stacks of hay and the old ones that had been carried over from the year before.

The desert beyond the rimrock on the other side of the Frying Pan seemed to go on and on forever, a gray vastness with a few ridges and buttes and rock pillars poking up into the horizon. The Lazy K was out there. For some reason which seemed entirely irrational, he thought of Cynthia and was pleased by the notion that she was in love with him.

The Lazy K meant something special to him. He had spent every Christmas there since he came to the Bar D. The Mayers never had any more presents than they'd had that first Christmas he'd been with them, but there was always an abundance of love in their home, and that made the difference between a Christmas on the Lazy K and one on the Bar D.

As long as he lived, he could never repay Bert Mayer. There were many things that put him in Bert's debt: taking him from Winnemucca in the first place, treating him as an equal, teaching him just as Ben Lampe had taught him when he'd stayed with Dora Lind.

Cynthia always made him welcome and never appeared to resent the extra work that his presence made for her. Pete went hunting with him and rode with him and worked with him, treating him as if he belonged to them. Even little Arnie, redheaded and big for his age, bellowing one moment because he had been punished and laughing the next, seemed to be happier because Tommy was there.

He shook his head, trying to put the Mayers out of his mind, and turned to look north at Indian and Skull Lakes, and Short Creek that connected them. Skull was gray and barren with very little swamp around it, for it had no outlet. Indian Lake was surrounded by thousands of acres of swamp covered with tules and cattails, with channels and islands that drove a man crazy if he got lost among them.

"Tommy."

Again he was jarred from his thinking by Bonnie's voice. When he looked at her, he realized he had been purposely trying to avoid thinking of her and how he felt about her and that this was the last afternoon they would spend together.

"You're a thousand miles away today," she said. "You're right here beside me, but you're not here. I've never seen you like this before."

"I guess I've never been like this. We'd better start back."

"No," she cried. "Not yet. Tommy, there's something we've got to talk about. I want you to know how I feel about dad."

"You don't need to tell me. I know how you feel. You're all he's got. He's given you everything he

96

could, and he'd give you more if you asked. Rose has told me a lot of times how he used to be different. She says your pa wanted a boy, but since he doesn't have one, you're all there is. That's why he'd never put up with me for a son-in-law. I guess I knew that all the time."

"That's not what I wanted to say. I know he's done things for me. He sent Rose and me to San Francisco a couple of times to buy clothes and see shows and everything. He's talked about putting me in a school, but I don't want that. He says Rose and I can go to Europe, but who wants to go to Europe?"

"I wouldn't, but—"

"Neither do I. Tommy, people hate him. Rose does too, even if he is her brother, and she makes herself miserable by staying on the Bar D and keeping house for him and looking after me when all the time she wants to marry Bert Mayer and live in that old shack of his."

"Why doesn't she?" Tommy asked.

"I don't know," she said. "Maybe they're cowards and it takes courage to stand up to dad. I guess I hate him too, but not for the same reasons. You say he's done everything for me and he'd do more; everything but what I want. Maybe you won't understand. It looks to you like I've got all anyone could want."

"Yeah, it sure does."

"Well, there's one thing he hasn't done and he never will. He'll never let me be myself. Whenever I wanted a new doll or a new dress or a horse, I got it, but I always knew he was giving it to me. I had to run when he got home and jump into his lap and kiss him and thank him for what he'd brought me."

She stopped, staring at him, then she cried out, "Marry me, Tommy. We don't always have to live under his thumb like a pair of dogs begging for something to eat."

"I can't," he said miserably, for he understood better than she knew. "You couldn't live the way I'll have to live, looking for a job and going hungry and drifting around. I love you too much to let you."

"And because dad would never change his mind about us," she said bitterly. "All right. I don't want to say good-by, but that's what this is."

She sat up and tried to smile, but she could not. She blinked against the tears that were in her eyes, then she lay down, patting the grass beside her. "Kiss me once more and then we'll go. Kiss me good and big so I'll always remember how it was."

He lay on his side and she came into his arms, her soft, yielding body clinging to his. The fire that was in her spread to him. He felt her need, and then his hunger for her swept away all restraints.

Afterwards he lay on his back, an arm thrown over his face, knowing that regret was the poorest of all human emotions. He had not intended to do this, but what was the use to tell Bonnie, or even to think it.

She tugged his arm away from his face and bending over him, kissed him. She said softly, "Now you've got to marry me. We'll tell dad tonight."

She laughed as she sat up and put a hand to her tousled hair, and it seemed to him she was proud and happy. "Tommy," she said, "for once I'll do something I want to do and dad will have to swallow his pride. I hope he chokes on it."

chapter 13

THEY RODE IN SILENCE down the mountain, the pleased and happy expression lingering on Bonnie's face, her head held high and proud. She had wanted him, and now, having had him, she was not in the least ashamed.

As she had said, he would have to marry her now. He was terrified by the prospect. It wasn't that he didn't want to marry her, but he was practical enough to know how Mike Dugan would take it.

Dugan wouldn't let him stay on the Bar D, and he couldn't take Bonnie with him. He would have to marry her and let her return to her home, and when he was settled and could take care of her, he'd send for her.

When they reached the house, she said, "Leave the horses saddled. Maybe I'll have to ride away with you." He dismounted and gave her a hand, thinking that she understood the seriousness of this. Then she said, "Let me do the talking. Dad won't get ornery if we don't make him mad." Then he knew he had been wrong, that she didn't understand how serious this was.

They walked through the row of poplars and across the yard, her arm through his. Suddenly he wanted to run. He was going to have to stand up to Mike Dugan, and he didn't know of anyone who had stood up to him and survived. Except Ben Lampe, and Ben had wound up losing both his job and his girl.

Then Tommy looked down at Bonnie. She hadn't lost her nerve. Not a bit of it. Well, he wouldn't, either. This wasn't going to be the way it had been yesterday when he'd sat his saddle and watched Dugan kick Corrigan.

They went into the house and along the hall and into the parlor. Rose was sitting beside the oak table reading. She glanced up when she heard them, her eyes going immediately to Bonnie's face. She stiffened, and started to get up, and fell back into her chair. *She knows,* Tommy thought. *She knows what happened just by looking at us.*

"Is dad home?" Bonnie asked.

They stopped, the table between them and Rose. Rose wet her lips with the tip of her tongue, and nodded. She said in a tone so low it was barely audible, "He's in his office."

"Please get him," Bonnie said.

Rose hesitated, her gaze going briefly to Tommy's face and returning to Bonnie's. She said, "I told you once today I knew your father better than you. Are you sure you want me to get him?"

"Yes, we're sure," Bonnie said.

Rose got up and left the room. Tommy heard her

voice, but he couldn't make out the words; then Dugan's rumble, "I'm busy." Rose said something else, and Dugan bellowed, "Gordon? His head must be solid bone. He sure can't get anything through it."

Dugan stomped into the room, Rose following. "So you want to see me, do you, Bonnie? All right, but I've got something to tell Gordon first. If you ever go anywhere with Bonnie again, I'll—"

"Listen to me," Bonnie interrupted. "We're going to get married."

"Married?" The word visibly jolted Dugan. Then he laughed, a derisive sound. "I wouldn't let you marry this pup if you were fifty years old and he was the only man left." He glowered at her, then asked, "What makes you think you're old enough to get married?"

"I'm a woman," Bonnie said. "I'm plenty old enough to get married, but I'll always be a child to you, even when I'm fifty."

Dugan's gaze swung to Tommy. "What kind of a cock-and-bull story have you been giving her?"

"Dad," Bonnie cried, "it's time you started realizing I'm not a child any more. You want to know why I think I'm old enough to get married. All right, I'll tell you. I'm old enough to have a baby, so I'm old enough to get married."

"What's she talking about?" Dugan whirled to face Rose. "You're a woman. You're responsible for her."

"No, Mike," she said. "You're responsible for her the same as you're responsible for everything that happens within a hundred miles of here."

"Nobody's responsible for me," Bonnie cried, angry now. "I'm old enough to be responsible for myself, but if you want your grandchild to have a name, you'll let us get married."

Startled, Tommy stepped away from Bonnie. Maybe she was pregnant, but she couldn't know whether she was or not. This was the worst possible way to approach Dugan. Tommy said. "Wait a minute, Bonnie. I—"

"Wait a minute, hell," Dugan bellowed. "You take her out in the brush and get her knocked up, and you say to wait a minute. Well, you'll wait, all right. You'll wait till I get my quirt."

Wheeling, Dugan stalked into his office. Rose grabbed at an arm, screaming at him, "No, Mike. Don't do it."

He raised a hand and struck her on the side of the face, a hard blow with the palm of his hand that sent her spinning. "Don't talk to me. You were supposed to keep an eye on her. You probably knew what was going on all the time."

He went on into the office. Bonnie, frightened now, took Tommy's arm. "We'll run off. That's all we can do if he's going to act like this."

He shook his head. "We can't run from him. Nobody can. We'll settle this now." He raised his voice, calling, "Dugan, we want your permission to get married. If we don't have it, we'll go away."

Dugan came back into the room carrying a quirt. "You won't go anywhere, you son of a bitch. I'll whip

102

you to death. She'll never have your brat and you'll never marry her."

Tommy drew his gun. He said, "If you lay that quirt on me, I'll kill you. I'm not Corrigan."

Bonnie ran between them, screaming, "Dad, can't you understand? I don't want you two to fight. Can't you see what you're doing to me?"

He caught her by an arm and whirled her around and forced her down on the black leather couch. "You don't know what you've done to me. You're a God-damned tramp, and all the time I thought I was raising a decent girl."

Rose held a hand to the side of her face where Dugan had struck her. She said, "Mike, for once try to think of someone besides yourself. What they've done isn't half as bad as what you did to Bert Mayer's wife. You're to blame for her death, and if you were any kind of a man, you'd take Arnie and raise him. He's your boy and you know it."

Dugan was trembling, his eyes not leaving Tommy's face for a moment. Spit ran down his chin. The slanting sunlight coming through the west windows glistened on his face, shiny with beads of sweat that had broken through his skin.

Dugan took a step toward Tommy, raising the quirt in a half-hearted manner as if not sure whether Tommy would do what he'd threatened or not. Or perhaps Rose's words took some of the maniacal fury out of him.

"One more step and I'll shoot you," Tommy said. "Seems funny to me, you saying Bonnie and me did something wrong. How many women have you done like you did Mrs. Mayer? Bonnie and me want to make it right, but you never even tried to make it right with Arnie."

Dugan's face turned purple. He threw the quirt on the floor. He said thickly, "I'll have you gelded. You'll never be able to get to another woman."

"No you won't," Rose cried. "If you do, I'll go to Bert. He's wanted to kill you for a long time. I've held him back, but if you do anything to Tommy, I'll help Bert kill you."

Dugan took two lurching steps to the couch and sat down beside Bonnie, dropping suddenly as if his knees could no longer hold his big body. He was having trouble breathing. He leaned forward, his great chest heaving as he struggled to suck air into his lungs.

"You'd better listen to me, Mike," Rose said. "Tommy walks out of here and you're giving me your word not to harm him. If you'll do that, Bonnie will stay. She doesn't really love Tommy. Not the way he loves her. She's using him against you, Mike. She just wants to be free, and this is the only way she could think of to get her freedom."

Tommy looked at Bonnie, waiting for her to deny what Rose had said. But the girl was staring at the floor, the pride and satisfaction that had been in her a few minutes before now completely gone.

"This is hard on you, Tommy," Rose said softly. "I'm sorry, but you've got to face the truth. Go away and forget her."

Tommy said, "Bonnie?"

"Go away," she said thickly. "Rose is right. I had to do something for myself, something important that dad didn't want me to do."

"You're not coming with me?"

"No." She looked at him briefly, then stared at the floor again. "You think I'd starve on a cow hand's wages when my father is the richest man in this part of the state?"

Still he stood there, staring at her. It couldn't be true, and yet, thinking back to what she had said on the mountain just before they started down, he knew it could be. Her words came back to him: *For once I'll do something I want to do and Dad will have to swallow his pride. I hope he chokes on it.*

So he had to go alone. This was another part of life behind him, another chapter closed that had been both wonderful and terrifying. But he couldn't spend the rest of his life running from Mike Dugan.

"How about it, Dugan?" Tommy said. "If we're going to fight, let's do it now."

Dugan was still having trouble with his breathing; his lips didn't function as they should and his words were thick when he said, "You've got twenty-four hours to leave the country. If you're not gone then, I'll take a knife to you."

Tommy turned and strode out of the house, not looking back. He felt like a man who had been awakened from a dream, knowing for the first time that it had been nothing more.

chapter 14

TOMMY RODE NORTH from the Bar D, unable to think coherently, or even to realize fully what had happened. All he could remember was that for a few brief moments up there on a shoulder of North Medicine Peak he had possessed Bonnie, that he had even been sure she loved him.

It was inconceivable that she could have given herself to him simply because she hated her father, simply to defy the man who had insisted on controlling her thoughts and affection and ambitions from the moment her mother had died.

Tommy glanced behind him often as he rode, his hand never far from gun butt, for he had no faith in Mike Dugan's promise that be would give Tommy twenty-four hours. He had no real purpose in mind; he only knew that he must be out of the country in twenty-four hours, that there was a chance Dugan would keep his word and give him that much time.

At dusk he reached a sage-covered ridge where the road made a wide arc around Indian Lake. He reined up to stare moodily out across the great expanse of tules and cattails, and at the black surface of water in the center of the swamp. Here was the home of swans and pelicans, of ducks and geese, of herons and the few snowy egrets that remained after the plume hunters had come.

He sat his saddle there a long time while dusk turned

to night and the cold stars came out. He listened to the night birds, to the first call of the coyotes from the barren ridges to the east that ran northward from the Two Medicine Peaks range.

He thought about Dugan who had spent so much effort clearing the swamp along the Frying Pan and turning it into hay land. Before long Marvin Gentry's Wineglass would become part of Mike Dugan's empire. Then Dugan would move his fence north so that it crossed Indian Valley. In time he would drain Indian Lake and burn off the tules and turn this swamp into hay land.

Tommy rode on toward Starbuck, the road swinging west again and going past Wineglass, lamp light in the windows of Gentry's ranch house visible to him. He thought of going in and warning the man, then put it out of his mind. Gentry knew, but he was still helpless to avert what was going to happen to him.

That was the way with everyone who was in Dugan's way, Tommy thought. Rose. Bonnie. Bert Mayer, too. Tommy had suspected about little Arnie's parenthood, for there had been hints in the talk Tommy had heard. Now he was sure. Dugan hadn't even denied it.

Tommy didn't understand Bert Mayer. He wasn't a coward. Tommy remembered what Ben Lampe had said about him a long time ago in Winnemucca: "He's cold turkey when it comes to a fight. I've seen him kill two men and he didn't turn a hair."

But how else could his behavior be explained, still

living on the Lazy K within twenty miles of the Bar D, still carrying on a partnership of sorts with the man who had seduced his wife, the man who was the father of a child Mayer was raising as his own? There was an end to what any man could stand, and Mayer must have reached it a long time ago.

Now the thoughts were churning in Tommy's mind. He was remembering what Eddie Vance had said yesterday afternoon. Vance claimed he was a free man, that he would not ignore the day when the farmers were forced off their land. This day was as good as any. The Corrigan case was clear-cut, brutal and completely illegal. Eddie Vance would have his chance.

Not a light showed in Starbuck when Tommy reached the edge of town, the false-fronted buildings standing tall and dark in the starlight. Tommy reined to the left and coming to the rear of the store, rode past it and came to the shack which housed Eddie Vance's print shop. He lived in a single room in the rear.

Tommy dismounted and knocked on the back door. Presently a match flared inside and Vance called, "All right. All right. Leave the damned door on its hinges." He lighted a lamp and a moment later opened the door and peering into the darkness, called out, "Who is it?"

"Me," Tommy said, and stepped into the shaft of light.

"Oh hell," the newspaper man muttered. "You."

"I've got a story for you," Tommy said. "You'd better be glad to see me."

"I'm tickled to death," Vance said. "Come in." He yawned and rubbed his eyes. "I was dreaming about women. It's the best I can do in this town. Just dream about them, and you wake me up. Couldn't this story wait till morning?"

"No," Tommy said, and sat down on the one straight-backed chair in the cluttered room.

Vance was in his underwear, his scant hair standing on end, a two-day stubble showing on his face. He was a skinny man, his gray eyes red and bleary as if he'd been on a twenty-four hour binge, but he was sober enough. He didn't look much like a hero, Tommy thought, just a middle-aged, tramp newspaper man who had started his business here because no one else had.

Vance filled his pipe, yawned, and rubbed his face. "All right," he mumbled around the pipestem as he touched a match flame to the tobacco. "Let's have it."

"I've quit the Bar D," Tommy said, "Or been fired, whichever way you want to say it."

"Depends on who says it," Vance said.

"Sure." Tommy nodded. "I've been given twenty-four hours to get out of the country, and I aim to be out when the time's up. Yesterday you were talking about being a free man and not belonging to Dugan. I'm wondering if it was just hot air."

"It wasn't," Vance said sharply. "Let's have your tale."

"In a minute. I want to know if the Corrigans are in town."

Vance nodded and chewed on his pipestem. "They're bedded down in their wagon back of the hotel. Didn't have any money, Mrs. Corrigan said, so didn't get a room."

"What shape's Corrigan in?"

Vance sat down on his crumpled bed, scowling. "How'd you come to know about it?"

"I'll tell you in a minute."

"Well, Corrigan's in a hell of a shape. About half conscious. Keeps mumbling about Dugan, but you can't get what he's trying to say."

"Did Mrs. Corrigan tell what happened?"

"No." Vance scratched the bald spot on his head. "Kind of queer, now that I think about it. Corrigan kept trying to talk about Dugan and she kept shushing him up. Wanted to get rid of me too, looked like. Finally she said they're going to pull out soon as doc says her husband can travel."

"Here's your story," Tommy said, "I'm going to be mighty interested in hearing whether you'll print it or not."

He told Vance what had happened, ending with, "I could have stopped it, maybe, but I didn't try, so I'm not proud of myself. I figured this was the least I could do. Folks hereabouts ought to know what Dugan is and how he operates."

Vance's pipe had gone cold in his hand. He squinted at Tommy as he reached for a match on the upended box that held a lamp beside the head of the bed. "Won't do a bit of good, son. Broncho Quinn wouldn't arrest Dugan. Besides, folks won't take up a fight with Dugan on account of a family like the Corrigans that are leaving the country."

"Are you going to print the story?"

"No."

"Well, by God," Tommy said softly. "That was just bull you were giving me yesterday. A free man, hell."

Vance's face turned red. "You're talking big for a gent who's leaving the country. How come Dugan gave you twenty-four hours?"

"That's got nothing to do with the Corrigans," Tommy said. "I wasn't doing the bragging yesterday how I'd buck Dugan."

"I wasn't, either, if you remember what I said," Vance shot back. "Look, boy. We've been friends for quite a while. I always figured you wouldn't stick because you're cut from a different bolt of cloth than Todd Moody for instance. But the reason I'm not printing your story isn't what you think it is. I'd do it if I was sure of my ground."

"I've told you—"

"Look at it my way," Vance interrupted. "You're telling me what happened, but you won't be around to verify it when Dugan's asking me for proof. And Mrs. Corrigan won't open her mouth."

"Why?" Tommy demanded. "She was yelling at Dugan that she'd tell the sheriff."

"She thought it over and changed her mind, looks like," Vance said. "All she wants is to get out of the country. She's smart at that. She and the boy could wind up dead."

Tommy rose, knowing that Vance was perfectly right. Dugan controlled the law, so he was above it. Public opinion would not touch him. Vance's puny effort would only bring Dugan's wrath down upon his head.

"So long, Eddie," Tommy said.

"Good luck, boy," Vance called after him. "Someday you'll come back."

"The hell I will," Tommy said. "I'm like Mrs. Corrigan. All I want is to get out of the country."

"You'll be back," Vance said. "I hope I'm here when you do. Then we'll see."

Tommy didn't say anything more. No use. Eddie Vance could wait for him until he rotted. Let Mike Dugan own the country and everybody in it. There was a lot of world that wasn't in Indian Valley or along the Frying Pan. That was the world Tommy Gordon was going to see.

The light in Vance's window died as Tommy mounted. He rode out of town, knowing exactly how Mrs. Corrigan felt.

chapter 15

AT DAWN Tommy reached the rimrock on the western side of Indian Valley, followed it for a mile or more until he found a break, then put his chestnut up the rock-strewn slope to the top. He rode south again, watching the day being born in the east. He caught the first sharp glint of sunlight on the rock spires and buttes in the desert to the west; he saw the dark shadow that lay upon the valley slowly fade and the distant hills to his left turn brown and gold and saw the color die. Then the Lazy K lay directly in front of him.

Everyone in the family was eating breakfast except Arnie. This morning, as usual, he had gulped his breakfast and raced outside again. He was the first to see Tommy riding in. He helled, "Tommy's coming. Tommy's coming," jumping up and down in his excitement.

They rushed out through the back door, Pete and then Cynthia and finally Bert because age was slowing him up. When Tommy dismounted, Arnie ran to him, and Tommy picked him up and held him above his head while the boy kicked and screamed at the top of his voice, "Where'd you come from, Tommy? Where'd you come from?"

"Starbuck," Tommy said, and put Arnie down.

He thumped Pete on the back and Pete thumped him in return. He shook hands with Bert, and turned to Cynthia who remained behind the others, a little shy as she always was when he first came. He put an arm out and pulling her to him, hugged her and was a little surprised when she reached up and, drawing his head down, kissed him on the lips; then she backed away, blushing.

"Come on in," Cynthia said. "We were just eating breakfast."

"What are you doing here this time of morning?" Bert asked. "Been riding all night?"

"Almost," Tommy said as he followed them into the kitchen. "I left Bar D yesterday afternoon, rode into

113

Starbuck and got Eddie Vance out of bed, then headed here."

"You crazy thing," Cynthia scolded. "I suppose you didn't have any supper and you didn't sleep a wink."

"You suppose right," Tommy said. "I'm hungry, too."

"I should think so," Cynthia said. "I'll fry some eggs."

Tommy sat down at the table, Cynthia pouring a cup of coffee for him. Bert and Pete finished their breakfast, and Arnie, bored now that the excitement of Tommy's unexpected coming was over, ran outside again.

None of the Mayers said anything for a time, all three sensing that something was wrong but not wanting to pry. Tommy finished his coffee and Cynthia filled his cup again. Suddenly he realized he was tired and sleepy, and a kind of weary contentment took hold of him. These were his people, this was where he belonged, as much of a home as he had anywhere, and an almost overpowering urge to stay here possessed him. He would be welcome, he knew, but he couldn't.

"I'm out of a job," Tommy said. "I'm fired, or I quit, whichever way you want to say it."

"We'll say you quit," Bert said. "It was bound to come."

Pete, the most violent one in the family, demanded, "What'd that son of a bitch of a Dugan do to you?"

Cynthia brought the plate of eggs to Tommy, saying to Pete, "Let him eat his breakfast first."

He couldn't talk about Bonnie, Tommy thought, so

114

he'd tell about Corrigan and let it go at that. He finished with Dugan hitting him and Todd Moody holding his gun on him, and added, "So I figured it was time to roll my soogans."

"What'd you go to Starbuck for?" Pete asked.

"To talk to Eddie Vance. I thought if he knew what had happened, he'd print the truth, but he wouldn't."

"You can't blame him," Bert said.

An uneasy silence settled upon them as Tommy drank his third cup of coffee. He hadn't been here for months, neglect that was inexcusable. Bert was grayer than ever and a little stooped, looking years older than he was. Pete at eighteen was a taut length of rawhide making a valiant effort to grow a mustache. He was filled with restless energy that broke out at unexpected times and in unexpected ways. He wouldn't stay home much longer.

Tommy's gaze settled on Cynthia's face and he discovered that she had been looking at him. She glanced away quickly, embarrassed because he had caught her staring at him, but in the brief moment he had surprised her, he glimpsed something he had never seen on her face before. He was bothered by it, for he remembered Bonnie saying Cynthia was in love with him. Now he wondered if it was true.

Cynthia was plain; compared to Bonnie at least. She was wearing a faded house dress that fitted her trim body like a sack. She never took time to do anything with her hair. Now, thinking about it, Tommy realized she wasn't plain at all.

The trouble with Cynthia was the way she lived,

here on an isolated ranch where she seldom saw anyone. She hadn't been in Winnemucca for three years, and she had been in Starbuck only once since the town was started.

If Rose quit the Bar D and married Bert, she'd do something for Cynthia, but he doubted that she would ever actually marry Bert.

Bert rose. "Pete, better get that salt over to Barker's Spring. Tommy, why don't you go to bed for a while?"

"I'll be all right," Tommy said, and followed Bert and Pete outside.

Arnie had captured a grasshopper, and when he saw Tommy, he yelled, "Look. This old hopper's spitting tobacco juice."

Tommy stopped and admired the grasshopper's effort, then went on toward the corral, leaving Arnie to tear the hopper's legs from his body. After Pete rode off, Tommy said, "There's a little more to tell."

"I figured there was," Bert said.

"Bonnie and me were going to get married," Tommy said. "When we told Mike, he went clean crazy. Got a quirt and would have used it on me if I hadn't pulled a gun on him. Then he was going to make a gelding out of me, and Rose said you'd kill him if he did. She said she'd been holding you off. I don't guess that stopped him, but he finally agreed to give me twenty-four hours to get out of the country."

Bert stood motionless, staring off across the desert. Then he lighted his pipe, his motions slow and deliberate, and said, "Go on."

116

"That's about the size of it, except it seems that Bonnie didn't love me after all. Said she wouldn't live on a cow hand's wages. Rose claimed she was using me to hit at her father, doing something she wanted to do that he didn't want her to. Does that make any sense, Bert?"

"Lots of sense. She's had her way in a lot of little things, even something pretty big like you staying there. Mike didn't want you there, you know, but Bonnie would have raised hell if he'd fired you, so he's let it rock along, figuring you'd slope out someday, which you're doing."

The pipe had gone cold in Bert's hand. He went on, "I can see him blowing up when you two talked about getting married. Mike will never like the man she marries, but for you to even think about it . . ." Bert shook his head. "Bonnie wanted something big to rebel about. Well, I guess she found it."

Bert didn't know how big it had been, Tommy thought. He wanted to say something about Dugan being Arnie's father, and knew at once it would be the worst thing he could say. Bert must hate himself every time he thought about it, and there were probably few waking moments when he wasn't thinking about it.

Impulsively Tommy laid a hand on Bert's shoulder. "Marry Rose. You've wasted years of both your lives."

"I know," Bert said somberly. "She figured she was obligated because of Bonnie. You've busted everything up there, so now maybe she'll come to me." He took his pipe out of his mouth and stared at it. "Tommy, do you really love Bonnie?"

Tommy turned away. He didn't know, so he couldn't answer the question, and it bothered him that he hadn't been hurt more than he had by Bonnie's refusal to go with him. The truth was he felt relieved and he didn't understand it.

"I've need to get some things sorted out, Bert," Tommy said finally. "Right now I've got to go away."

"You can stay with us," Bert said. "We'll fight Dugan if it comes to that."

"No, I'd just bring trouble to all of you. I'm not sure where I'll go. Maybe back to see Aunt Sadie. I know damned well she robbed me. Time I was doing something about it."

There was silence for a moment. Then Bert said quietly, "All right, boy. But write to us. You hear?"

"I'll write."

"You'll come back. Just don't wait too long."

Tommy turned, remembering that Eddie Vance had said the same thing. Well, they were both wrong. He said, "I don't figure to be back, Bert," and went on to the house.

Cynthia was washing dishes in the kitchen when he stepped through the back door. She looked at him, smiling, and he wondered why he had thought she was plain. There was a bright and shiny look about her that set her apart from other women.

"More coffee, Tommy?" she asked.

"No. I came to tell you good-by. I'm leaving the country."

She dropped the plate she was holding. It splashed water out of the pan as it fell. Slowly she turned to the towel that hung on the wall and dried her hands, then she went to him, the bright look gone from her.

"Write to us," she said.

She stood in front of him, her head tipped back, and then her control broke and she hugged him frantically, her head pressed against his chest. "Don't go, Tommy. Don't go. You belong to us. You always have. You never belonged to the Bar D."

"I guess that's right," he said, "but I've got to go."

He kissed her and she clung to him, then she stepped away, her face composed. "Good-by, Tommy," she said. "God bless you always."

Bert had his horse waiting for him. He shook hands, saying nothing. When he rode away, Cynthia was standing beside the house watching. She was still there when he disappeared over the next ridge.

chapter 16

TOMMY RODE SOUTH, keeping well to the west of Bar D range and the neighboring ranches like Jim Becker's Mule Ear. He followed Warner Valley for a time, crossed into Nevada and turned east, keeping north of the Black Rock Desert. He struck Quinn River and swung south again, the country vaguely familiar to him. He wasn't far from the route Bert Mayer and he had taken nearly five years ago.

He rode into Winnemucca late that afternoon. The

119

town hadn't changed: the tracks, the shipping pens, the depot, and the business blocks where he had made his search for work the morning after he'd stepped off the train. Memories crowded back into his mind, and suddenly he was filled with a great hunger to see Ben Lampe and Dora Lind again.

The five years might have been five days as far as the appearance of the town was concerned, but the people had changed. At least he saw no one he knew. A lanky man was leaning against the wall of the jail, a star on his vest. He sharpened a match, his gaze on Tommy as he rode past, then began picking his teeth, apparently dismissing the dusty chestnut and the buckaroo with the stubble-covered face as being just another drifter and his horse that would be gone tomorrow. No Ben Lampe, that one, Tommy thought.

Tommy turned into Thorne's stable and dismounted. A clubfooted hostler limped toward him. "Thorne here?" Tommy asked.

"Getting supper," the hostler said. "He'll be back in half an hour or so."

"I'll wait," Tommy said.

He rubbed Slats down, saw to it that the chestnut was given a double bait of oats, and then stood in the archway smoking a cigarette until Alec Thorne returned. The liveryman didn't know Tommy for a time. He shook the proffered hand, eyes moving up and down Tommy's long body and finally coming to rest on the dust-caked, whiskered face. Then it struck him, and he grabbed Tommy's hand and shook it again and slapped him on the back.

"You're the kid that rode north with Bert Mayer," Thorne shouted. "Stayed with Dora Lind. Ben Lampe kind o' looked out for you. You wanted to sign on with Mike Dugan and he didn't want no part of you."

Thorne stepped back and scratched the bald spot on the top of his head. "Tommy. Tommy Gordon. That's it. Growed up to be quite a man. Let's see now, that was two, no, three years ago, wasn't it."

"Five, come fall," Tommy said.

"Hell, time sure gets away from a man. Five years. Yeah, guess it was, now that I think about it. That's how long Ben's been gone."

"Where is Ben?"

Thorne acted as if he didn't hear. "Come on in, boy. I've got me a bottle of good stuff I save for special occasions."

Tommy followed Thorne into his office. "Where is Ben?" he asked again.

Thorne pretended he didn't hear the question this time either. He opened a drawer of his desk and took out a bottle. He pulled the cork, rubbed a sleeve across the mouth, and handed the bottle to Tommy. Tommy took a pull on it, then gave it back to Thorne, who took a drink and set it on the desk.

"Where you been, Tommy?" Thorne asked. "Sit down and tell me about yourself."

"You're going to answer my question," Tommy said.

Thorne sat down at his desk. He pointed to an upended box and sighed. "Thought a lot of Ben, didn't you, boy?"

"A hell of a lot," Tommy said.

"I hate to tell you," Thorne said, "but Ben's dead. A lot of us felt the same way you do. He was the best marshal this burg ever had."

"Dugan kill him?"

"Hell no. I ain't sure Dugan was man enough to do it. No, Ben turned in his star just after you left and took a train to Reno. He drifted south and got a marshal's job in a mining camp. I reckon we never did get the whole story, but from what we heard, he ran into a gunslinger who liked to cut notches on his gun. Ben never was very fast, you know."

Tommy nodded and was silent for a moment. He wasn't surprised, and wasn't sure why unless it was a sense of destiny. Dugan had killed Ben as surely as if he had pulled the trigger. If Dugan had let Dora alone, Ben would have married her and settled down in Winnemucca and been alive today. After what had happened, he probably hadn't cared much either way.

"Funny thing about Ben," Thorne said thoughtfully. "He was big and strong, and he sure had his share of guts, but—"

"Dora?' Tommy interrupted. "What happened to her?"

"The last I heard, she was running a millinery store in Rawlins, Wyoming." Thorne picked up a pipe from his desk and filled it. "You know, folks always liked Dora and figured she'd marry Ben, but after what hap-

122

pened between her and Dugan. . . ." He shrugged. "Well, Dugan always has had a way about him."

"When did she leave?" Tommy asked.

"Right after Ben did. Just walked out and left her store. She must have figured on Dugan marrying her, but hell, he don't have to account to either God or man, I guess."

"Thinks he doesn't anyway," Tommy said, and got up and walked to the door.

"Hold on, son," Thorne called. "Where you been all this time? What's happened to you?"

"Nothing," Tommy said. "I haven't been anywhere." That night he got drunk and the next morning left town with a head too big for his hat.

He kept on riding east, taking his time and not really sure what he wanted to do. He avoided saloons, knowing he would get drunk again, for the urge to forget Mike Dugan and everything he had done was a compelling need in him.

But he didn't really want to forget, he told himself. Both Eddie Vance and Bert Mayer had told him he would come back to Indian Valley, and at the time he hadn't believed them. Now he wondered.

He didn't understand Dugan. He doubted that anyone did. It was as Rose had often said. You had to take him the way he was. He couldn't keep from thinking about Ben Lampe, capable of handling almost anything and anybody except Dugan. Of Bert Mayer who had lost his wife because of Dugan. Of Corrigan who might be dead by now. And always his thoughts came back to Bonnie. He still found it hard to believe what Rose had said, what Bonnie herself had almost admitted, that she had used him as a weapon against her father. She loved him, Tommy told himself. He had to believe that.

He rode day after day with love and hatred as mixed in his mind as eggs in a breakfast omelet. In early September he reached Ogden. Drifting, he finally decided he'd head for Rawlins and see if he could find Dora. He wasn't certain what he'd say or what good he could do, but it was something he must do. She was at least in part to blame for Ben's death. If she didn't know it, it was time she was told.

Yet, as he left the mountains and crossed the barren and desolate plain that was much of southern Wyoming, he wasn't sure he would tell her. You couldn't live the past over, you couldn't rectify your mistakes. Maybe that was what held Bert Mayer back. Maybe it was the reason Mrs. Corrigan wouldn't stay in Indian Valley and tell what Dugan had done. Maybe knowledge of the past was punishment enough. Dora Lind certainly had that.

chapter 17

WHEN TOMMY REACHED RAWLINS, he put his horse in the first livery stable he saw and immediately asked for Dora Lind. The hostler spit a brown stream against the wall and tongued his quid to the other side of his mouth. "Hell, man," he said. "I'm married. If I set out to know every woman in this town, I'd get my throat cut."

"The last I heard of her, she was running a millinery store," Tommy said. "I don't think this burg's big enough to have many millinery stores."

The hostler squinted at Tommy as he rocked back on his heels. "You're right about that. Well sir, far as I know, there's two. One of 'em is yonder on Main Street. It's respectable. Belongs to a woman named Sandra Mason. The other one's next to the whore houses. A woman calling herself Mary Jones runs it."

"I'll have a look," Tommy said, and left the stable.

Maybe Dora had changed her name, he thought, as he strode toward Sandra Mason's store. She was a long ways from Winnemucca, but perhaps she thought she hadn't gone far enough to keep the story of what had happened in Winnemucca from following her here. Or she might be doing something else. Or she might not even be here. If she wasn't, he would probably never see her again, for this was the only hint he had as to where she was.

Sandra Mason wasn't Dora. She was a middle-aged, fat woman who insisted she had the only millinery shop in Rawlins. He left her store, turned right, and a moment later reached the tracks. Here, strung out for two blocks or more, were saloons and brothels. At the end of the second block he passed a row of cribs. Women were standing in doorways or sitting beside open windows, smiling their invitation to him.

Several of the women called to him, "Come on in,

honey. The service is good." Or, "You're passing up the best, honey. I know how to take care of a man." One grabbed for his hat and almost got it, and he heard the run of ribald laughter behind him. After that he walked on the edge of the sidewalk next to the street.

He paused at an intersection while a dray loaded with beer barrels rumbled past, then went on. After passing a saloon and vacant lot, he came to Mary Jones's millinery shop, a long narrow building set close to the sidewalk.

The front of the store was badly weathered, with little of the paint left that had been given it years ago. The windows were dirty and decorated with countless cobwebs. When he opened the door, a sheep bell hanging directly above it gave out a metallic clang.

"Just a minute," a woman called from a back room. It was Dora's voice.

He stood motionless, appalled by the room that apparently had not been dusted for weeks. The only furnishings were a long counter with two hats perched on tall uprights, both gay with long curled plumes, one bright red, the other blue, and two straight-backed chairs. He remembered how spic and span Dora's place in Winnemucca had been.

A moment later she parted the curtain that covered the doorway in the rear of the room. When she saw a man standing there, she said sharply, "You've got the wrong place, mister. The girls you're looking for are up the street."

He didn't move. She was as slim as ever, holding

126

herself straight-backed the way he remembered, but the youth and beauty that he had admired were gone. Her hair was a dull, graying brown, and was drawn tightly back from her forehead and pinned in a bun. Time had carved deep lines around her eyes, and the skin of her cheeks and the curve of her jaw was like crepe.

She wore a black dress that fitted her perfectly, but was shiny with wear and frayed around the neck. The years and poverty had taken their toll, but she was clean and neat, and she carried herself with the same pride of body he remembered so well. At least she had not lost everything, he thought.

He walked slowly toward her. She shrank against the curtain, saying, "I told you—"

"Dora," he said. "Don't you know me?"

"Tommy." The name broke out of her parted lips, then the old familiar smile was there, and she cried out, "Oh, Tommy, Tommy, why didn't you tell me who you were?"

"I thought you'd know me," he said, and held out his arms to her.

She ran to him and he kissed her, and he held her hard for a moment, and then she put her head against his chest and began to cry. He felt like crying, too. He could not remember when he had felt this way. He wasn't sure why for a moment, then he thought he did. Ben Lampe was in the room with them, Ben Lampe who was dead, and in that moment Tommy knew that no matter how long he lived or what happened to him, no one would ever take the place in his heart that Ben Lampe and Dora Lind had once held.

She drew back, and finding a handkerchief, wiped her eyes. "I'm not a chronic cryer, Tommy," she said, "but I just couldn't help it. I've thought about you so many times and wondered what happened to you, but I never heard."

"I rode out of Winnemucca that night with Bert Mayer," he told her, "figuring I was going to work for him, but I wound up on the Bar D."

She frowned. "I hoped you wouldn't," she said. "I knew you wanted to, but I didn't think Mike Dugan was good for you."

"He wasn't," Tommy said. "He's not good for anybody."

She pretended she didn't hear. "You were a boy when you left, but you're a man now." She put a hand to his stubble-covered face. "Like barbed wire." She shook her head as if the changes in him were miraculous, then she laughed. "Oh Tommy, this is wonderful. I tell you what. I've got a little work to do on a hat. It'll take me about an hour. Why don't you go get a shave and buy a couple of T-bones and I'll cook supper for you. I'm a good cook. Remember?"

"I'll never forget," he said, and turned to the door.

"Be back in an hour," she said, and then, just as he put his hand on the knob, she asked, "You don't have a hotel room, do you?"

"No. I started looking for you as soon as I got into town."

"Good," she said. "Stay here with me tonight. There's nothing in Rawlins to keep a man like you, so I'm sure you won't need a hotel room. I don't want to lose a minute with you. I want to hear everything that's happened."

He hesitated, his hand still on the knob. She laughed shortly. "Don't worry about my reputation. When you live this close to the tracks, you don't have one."

"All right," he said. "I'll be back in an hour."

He was, shaved and bathed and wearing a clean shirt, with two big T-bones wrapped in butcher paper. She parted the curtains as soon as she heard the sheep bell. She had changed into a red-and-white checked house dress and was wearing a frilly apron. Her smile was quick and full, and her face showed the happiness that his presence brought to her.

"Come on back," she said, and led him through her work room with its table and chair and faded orange divan. It was clean, and so was the kitchen which was the next room. "I don't bother to keep the room next to the street clean," she explained. "There's so much dust from the street and cinders from the trains that go by all the time. It doesn't make any difference to the girls who come here."

She motioned to the table that was set with her best china and silver, and with two tall glass candlesticks in the center. "Sit down, Tommy," she said. "I'll start these streaks to frying."

He dropped into a chair and rolled a cigarette, noting that she moved with the quick grace he remembered.

129

It was as if his presence had rolled the years off her shoulders. She spooned grease into a frying pan, dropped the steaks into it, and moved it to the front of the stove.

"I've got biscuits in the oven and the potatoes are boiling," she said: "All I've got to do is to fry these steaks and make gravy. The coffee's about done. Why don't you go ahead and tell me about yourself."

Strange, he thought, how the old intimacy returned here within the warmth of her kitchen, and how his bitter thoughts about her were entirely gone from his mind. He could not in any way blame her for Ben Lampe's death. If Ben could not hold what belonged to him, he was to blame and Tommy could not fasten it upon Dora.

So he talked, loud enough to be heard over the sizzling steak and sparing none of the truth about Mike Dugan. But he could not bring himself to tell her what had happened on the shoulder of North Medicine Peak. He simply let her know that Dugan had exploded when he and Bonnie told him they wanted to get married.

She set the food on the table and then stood across from him, looking down and smiling at him. "Tommy, you really haven't changed so much. Now that you're shaved, I can see that. It's just that you're so much a man and you were a boy when you left Winnemucca." She sat down and passed him the meat platter. "I can't tell you how wonderful it is to have you here. It's like, well, like you had brought my youth back."

"You couldn't be more than twenty-six," he said, a small sense of shock in his mind.

She nodded. "I guess it comes down to the way you feel, not the years you've lived."

She ate with what seemed to Tommy a ravenous appetite. He suspected that it had been a long time since she had eaten a T-bone steak. Afterwards he helped her with the dishes, and she joked about how he'd had to do the dishes so much when he had lived with her.

When they were done, they sat down at the table again, filled coffee cups in front of them, a bracket lamp on the wall by the stove and the candles on the table the only light in the room.

"How do you feel about Bonnie now?"

"Nothing." And he realized as he said it that it was true. "No man likes to be made a fool of. Rose was right about her, I guess."

"What are you going to do?"

"Look up Aunt Sadie. She's got money that's coming to me. Maybe I can get some of it back. If I do, I'm coming here and taking you out of this mess. Wouldn't take much money to get you started again, would it?"

"No. Just a few hundred dollars."

"I'm coming back anyhow," he said. "You can't stay here."

"It's a living," she said. "I make their hats and, once in a while, a dress. I do some laundry for them. They're not bad women as most people call them. If you talk to them about their business, they'd say it's just as essential as the restaurant business, for instance. The morals of some repectable women are no better. Mine aren't. It's just that I couldn't do it for money. With me it would have to be because of what a man was and how much I thought of him."

She got up, suddenly restless, and walking to the stove, stood with her back to it, her eyes on Tommy. "I knew what Mike was, what he always will be. Maybe he was different once like his sister told you, but I don't believe it. I think he was always that way, and I think his girl will be the same, taking whatever she wants and never giving a damn about what she does to other people."

She took the lamp down from the bracket. "We'd better go to bed," she said. "I'll lock the front door."

In the morning after breakfast when he was ready to leave, she said, "Don't come back to me, Tommy. I can take care of myself and I know you can take care of yourself. And don't go back to destroy Dugan. You'll only destroy yourself if you do."

"You can't stay here," he said. "I want—"

"No," she said. "It's better to leave it this way."

A few minutes later he rode out of town, not sure that she was right, knowing only that he wanted to help her, and understanding some things he had never understood before. Ben Lampe, for all of his strength and courage, must have been the most frustrated and unhappy of all men.

chapter 18

AN EARLY FALL STORM caught Tommy three miles short of Prairie City. He stayed the night at a ranch. When he asked about Sadie Gordon, the rancher and his wife shook their heads. They knew the woman who ran the boarding house and her name wasn't Sadie Gordon.

The next morning Tommy rode to town through the heavy, wet snow. He didn't have much luck asking for Sadie. The woman who had bought the boarding house didn't know where she was. She said spitefully, "All I know is I paid too much. If you find her, tell her she robbed me."

"I can't tell her if I can't find her," Tommy said.

"I just don't know where she is," the woman said. "If I did, I'd tell you."

None of the railroad men knew, either. One of them said, "Sold out and left before I knowed she was even thinking about it. Not long after you pulled out, if I recollect right."

That's the way it would have been, Tommy thought bitterly. He had sold out for a few dollars, and once she was rid of him, she had seen no reason to go on working. Thinking back, Tommy could not blame himself. He had hated the country, the flat, endless prairie with its grass and wind and no trees. He still did. He wouldn't stay here any longer than he had to, Aunt Sadie or no Aunt Sadie. But he had every reason to blame her. What kind of a woman would rob a boy, stealing money that had been made by a dead brother and belonged to his son?

Near evening he talked to a woman who told him to see old lady Cartwright. "She was Sadie Gordon's only friend hereabouts," the woman said. "Why they liked each other I'll never know, but they did. If anyone can tell you where Sadie is, I guess old Mrs. Cartwright can."

He should have thought of her at first, Tommy reflected. Mrs. Cartwright was a recluse, a widow who lived up the track about a mile from the boarding house. More than once Aunt Sadie had sent him trudging along the dusty road with some tidbit for her. The trouble was that Mrs. Cartwright, being Aunt Sadie's friend, might suspect why he wanted to find her and would refuse to tell him where Aunt Sadie was even if she knew.

Before he reached Mrs. Cartwright's house, Tommy thought of a trick that might work, if the woman didn't recognize him, and he doubted that she would. No one else who had known him five years before had recognized him. Besides, it was dusk now, and he remembered that Mrs. Cartwright was nearsighted.

The old lady peered at him when she came to the door, saying with asperity, "Young man, if you're trying to sell me something, you're wasting your time."

"No ma'am," Tommy said. "I'm trying to get some information concerning the whereabouts of Sadie Gordon."

"I don't know nothing about her," Mrs. Cartwright said spiritedly, and slammed the door. Then she jerked it open and peered at Tommy again. "What's your name, young man, and what do you want Sadie Gordon for?"

"My name is Lawrence Harrison," Tommy said. "My business is strictly confidential, but you would be doing her a favor if you would tell me where I could find her."

"What kind of a favor?" Mrs. Cartwright asked suspiciously.

"I can't tell you that," Tommy said, "but I can say it would be to her financial advantage."

Mrs. Cartwright's interest perked up considerably at that. She said, "Now see here, young man. If you want to locate her, you'd best tell me what you want with her."

"Then you know where she is?"

"I know, all right. I visited her last spring, but I ain't going to have you bothering her and trying to get her money in some fool investment or sweet talking her into buying something she don't need. Now then, what do you want with her?"

Tommy took his time, pretending to think about it carefully, then she said, "Ma'am, all I want is to give her something. She had a brother who died several years ago in Missouri. The brother had a son who disappeared and is presumed to be dead. As far as we can determine, Sadie Gordon is the only heir."

"That's correct, young man," Mrs. Cartwright said.

"That son you're talking about was a rapscallion if there ever was one. Ran off from his Aunt Sadie after her giving him a home."

"We understand he was killed in a gun fight," Tommy said.

"Served him right." Mrs. Cartwright nodded with satisfaction. "Sadie will be glad to hear that."

"She'll hear it if I can find her," Tommy said. "You see, her brother had money in more than one bank. There is quite a sum in the bank in the town of Courtney which is a few miles from where he lived. I represent that bank. Before I left, I contacted Sherman Day. He was the lawyer who handled the estate. I understand that he worked with Sadie Gordon at the time of her brother's death, but he doesn't know where she is. If we can't locate her now, the bank will presume her dead, and if there are no other heirs, the money—"

"She lives in Cheyenne," Mrs. Cartwright interrupted. "I disremember the name of the street, but it's about three blocks east of the capitol building. You tell Sadie I sent you."

"I'll be happy to inform her," Tommy said. "Thank you."

He was halfway to his horse when Mrs. Cartwright called, "How much is it, young man?"

"$10,000," Tommy said, and went on.

"Land o' Goshen," Mrs. Cartwright marveled. "That's almost as much as she got in the first place."

Tommy mounted and rode away, laughing silently

when he thought how the promise of money and the mention of Sherman Day's name opened Mrs. Cartwright's mouth.

The laughter faded when he remembered Mrs. Cartwright had said that $10,000 was almost as much as Aunt Sadie had received in the first place. It must have been $14,000 or $15,000.

Two days later he was in Cheyenne. He located the capitol building, and from there rode three blocks east and found Aunt Sadie's house without any trouble, just as Mrs. Cartwright had said he would. She came to the door in answer to his knock, the rocking chair teetering back and forth behind her, a dish of fudge on the claw-footed stand beside the chair. She was massive, fifty pounds heavier than she had been five years before.

She stared at him blankly until he said, "Well, Aunt Sadie, it's wonderful to see your loving countenance again."

Her lips parted as color fled from her face. She backed up a step, a fat hand fluttering to her throat and dropping again. He saw that she was frightened, a discovery that gave him great satisfaction.

"I didn't know you, Thomas," she said, the tip of her tongue wetting her lips. She hesitated, then added, "Come in."

He opened the screen door and stepped into her parlor with its heavy, dark furniture and white curtains at the windows and an open Bible on the stand beside the lamp. Gold fringe hung from the shade on the lamp. He reached out and touched it.

"Gold, Aunt Sadie," he said. "Real gold from a Missouri bank and the sale of a good Missouri farm." He pointed to the Bible. "You live by the Word, don't you, Aunt Sadie? Serving God, but not Mammon. Isn't that right, Aunt Sadie?"

"Sit down, Thomas," she said, and dropped heavily into her rocking chair. "What do you want?"

"An accounting," he said.

"You left once," she said. "When you left, you gave up any right you had to an accounting."

"I'll have an accounting and don't you forget it." He told her how he had found her, adding, "I never knew exactly how much you got, but from what pa told me and from what Mrs. Cartwright said, it must have been between $15,000 and $20,000."

"No, no," she cried. "It wasn't that much. Not near that much. If that stupid Lizzie Cartwright hadn't . . ." She stopped, biting her lower lip. "All right, how much do you think you've got coming?"

"I suppose you deserve something for going back there," he said, "so I won't ask for all of it. I guess $10,000 would be about right."

She let out a screech like a stepped-on cat and cursed him. "That's ridiculous. None of it's yours by rights, but I'll give you $500 if you'll sign a paper not to bother me again. It's worth that much to get rid of you."

"My dear Aunt Sadie," he said softly. "You won't get rid of me that easy. I might even twist your fat neck."

"And hang," she said. "I knew your father too well to think his son would do anything of the sort. $500. How about it?"

He shook his head. "Looks like I'll have to go back to Missouri and see Sherman Day."

"No need of that," she snapped. "I'll make it $1,000."

"You're not dealing with a boy you scared out of his hide," he said, "but you'll make a reasonable settlement or I will go to Missouri, and I'll find out exactly how much you got from my father's estate, then I'll come back and go to the police. Maybe I'll bring Sherman Day with me. He was pa's friend and I think he'd come. I'll put you through every court in the country and you'll come out broke."

"It's worth something to get rid of you for good," she said. "I'll give you $1,500."

He shook his head. "I told you $10,000."

She sat glaring at him, but when he got up and started toward the door, she screamed, "$5,000. Not a cent more."

He turned, surprised at the size of the raise. "$9,000."

"No," she yelled. "$5,000, and I'll have to go to work again, with you robbing me like that."

"It'll take some fat off you," he said, and went on, getting to the door this time.

"$6,000. That's the ceiling."

With an extended hand on the screen, he looked back at her furious face, so dark red it was nearly purple. "$8,000. That's the floor."

"No, no, no."

He shoved the screen open and left the house. He got to his horse and stepped into the saddle, doubts crowding into him. He was whipped if he went back and offered to settle for $6,000. She'd know she had him scared and running, and she'd withdraw her offer.

On the other hand, he didn't have the money to take the case into court and fight it out. He had made one bet too many and had lost, he thought as he started to ride away.

Then she was at the door, yelling at him in her shrew voice, "All right, all right, you bastard. $7,000."

He reined up and looked back, thinking bitterly that of all the women in the world who could have been his one living relative, it had to be this mountain of flesh. He said, "I'll settle for that if you'll take care of it today."

"All right," she said. "As soon as I can get to the bank."

An hour later they completed the transaction in a lawyer's office. He signed a paper and took the money, and as he walked toward the door, she cursed him again. He turned, pitying her, and when she ran out of breath, he said, "Remember me in your will, Aunt Sadie."

He walked out without giving her time to take another breath and start cursing him again. He had dinner before he left town, thinking about Dora Lind. She hadn't wanted him to come back, she had said. She might be gone from Rawlins by now. She was older than he was and wiser, so she was probably right.

Indian Valley? When he'd left, he hadn't wanted to ever see it again, but he did now. He had ridden a lot of miles since he had left Oregon, a lot of things had happened to him, and suddenly he had a great desire to see Bert Mayer and Cynthia and Pete and little Arnie. Rose Dugan. Eddie Vance, too.

But he could not go back until he was ready to stand against Mike Dugan. Not destroy him necessarily. Dora Lind had been right about that. Bert would say the same. He would end up by destroying himself.

Still, it would be a fight, one way or another, and he wasn't ready for it yet. He wasn't sure what it took in a man, but he knew it was more than physical courage. Maybe it was a sense of assurance inside him. He knew that if men like Ben Lampe and Bert Mayer and Eddie Vance could not stand against Mike Dugan, he couldn't either. Maybe in time, but not now.

So he mounted and rode south toward Denver, not because there was anything for him in Denver, but he had never seen the city and he wanted to. He would winter there. And after that? He didn't know and at the moment didn't care. He might drift over the mountains and buy a ranch on the western slope. He'd heard it was good cattle country.

It was a comfortable feeling to realize he didn't have to make any immediate decisions. Time would take care of that. He would live tomorrow when it became today. He thought with satisfaction that there would be a great many tomorrows.

BOOK III   THE MAN

chapter 19

SUMMER AGAIN, and with the lush green floor of Indian Valley spread out before him, Tom Gordon told himself that five years could change a man, but not the face of nature. Sitting his saddle on the crest of hills that were the eastern boundary of Indian Valley, he thought he might have been gone five days instead of five years as far as the country was concerned.

Far across the vast, flat floor of the valley was the western rim, almost hidden by summer haze. On beyond the rim was the Lazy K. He'd reach it by night. Cynthia would be waiting for him. He'd written her as he'd promised he would. He'd heard regularly from her, and through the years an understanding had grown between them.

When he'd gotten settled on his Colorado ranch, he'd suggested the Mayer family come to live with him. But Bert wouldn't budge. So Tom was coming back to them. To little Arnie, eleven now and not so little. To Rose Dugan, or Rose Mayer, for she had married Bert four years ago. Only Pete was gone, working for an outfit on the Crooked River above Prineville.

His horse rested, Tom rode on down the slope, seeing Starbuck ahead of him and the settlers' shacks scattered to the north; unhealthy pimples on the face of the land, it seemed to Tom. Dugan had always claimed that farming wouldn't pay in the valley, with a short growing season and water as scarce as it was.

Dugan was right, Tom thought, just as he was right about a good many things. Even if Starbuck with its store and bank had been in the hands of a friendly man instead of Mike Dugan, the farmers would fail in the end.

He reached Starbuck about noon. He was hungry, for he hadn't eaten since sunup, but he wouldn't stop in Starbuck. Cynthia had written about a man named Andrew Hamilton who had started a new town on the other side of Duck River that he called Eula. He'd have his dinner there, but he refused to circle Starbuck, partly because he wanted to see if it had changed, but mostly because he would not admit to himself or to anyone that he was afraid to face Todd Moody or Lew Roman or Dugan himself.

He saw little change as he rode the length of Starbuck's dusty street. Finley's Bar, which had been the hangout of the settlers, was empty, the windows boarded up. So was Eddie Vance's print shop. As Tom rode by the courthouse, Broncho Quinn came out of the front door and stared at him as if trying to dredge up a memory from the dead past. Tom went on, his thoughts turned bitter. Quinn was wearing a star, so Dugan still controlled the sheriff's office.

Tom forded Duck River, the water shallow at this point as it ran over a muddy bottom. His horse, a leggy sorrel he'd traded for in the spring just after he sold his chestnut Slats, climbed the sloping west bank, snorting his disapproval.

Glancing at the hills to the north, Tom told himself he'd buy a ranch in that area. It was a better country than that east of the river. When he left, there had been a few scattered ranches in the northwest corner of the valley, the Diamond A and the Cross 9 he remembered. More now, probably. He had better than $10,000 in the money belt around his middle, the results of the sale of his Colorado ranch, more than enough to buy any of the small ranches in the valley.

Eula was directly ahead of him. Disappointment jolted him. He should have been warned, for Cynthia had written that almost no one traded here. Eula consisted of one false-fronted building on the south side of the street, a shed and pole corral behind it, and a small dwelling across the road, a woodshed and a privy to the rear of it. The rest of the town was nothing more than weed-grown lots on both sides of the road marked by tall stakes, a "For Sale" sign on every one of them. A dream! That was Eula. Irritated because he had expected more, Tom rode on, not even stopping to buy anything to eat.

The irritation grew in him as he rode. He had hoped this Andrew Hamilton who had built Eula would be an ally in his fight with Dugan, but the man was a dreamer. Tom would ask Bert about him, but it was unlikely that a man of Hamilton's caliber could be counted on when the chips were down.

Tom did not doubt that his return would force a fight

144

with Dugan. He had hated the man from the moment he had pushed Tom aside in Winnemucca when he'd asked for a job. Working for Dugan and then being away for five years had not changed or softened that hatred. Now he was back, with enough money and experience and self-confidence to stand up to Dugan.

He had told himself it was Cynthia who was bringing him back; that it was his love for her and the desire to return to his own people that had made him sell a good ranch in western Colorado and ride nearly a thousand miles.

He did love Cynthia and he intended to marry her, but now he knew it was more than this which had brought him back to Indian Valley.

Tom reached the Lazy K with the sun a red disc hanging just above the western rim. Arnie was the first to see him coming. The boy was chopping wood behind the house. He straightened, and sinking the ax into the chopping block, stared at Tom. He didn't know the sorrel horse, so he didn't recognize Tom until he dismounted. Then he saw who it was, and raced for him, whooping like an Indian.

Cynthia was the first one out of the house. She ran into Tom's arms, and lifting her mouth for his kiss, clung to him frantically as if resolved to never let him out of her sight again. Then he was shaking hands with Bert, kissing Rose, and tousling Arnie's hair, saying, "Boy, you sure have grown up since I left." Arnie, suddenly shy, grinned and didn't say anything. Tom had to turn his head to hide his expression, so shocked was he by Arnie's resemblance to Mike Dugan.

They were all talking at once. Cynthia, still clinging to an arm, said, "Come on in. We were just sitting down to supper." And Bert, "Put his horse up, Arnie." And Rose, "I declare, Tom, I think Cynthia knew you were coming. She's been primping all afternoon." Blushing, Cynthia said indignantly, "I wasn't, Rose. You know I wasn't."

Tom followed them into the house, a lump in his throat for the first time in years. He had stayed away too long. It was, as Cynthia had once said, this was where he belonged, these were his people.

Another lean-to room had been built on since Tom had been here, but aside from that, there was no change. No change outside, either, with the far reach of the dreary desert all around, the dust and sagebrush and occasional juniper, the upthrusts of barren lava and the distant buttes.

As Tom washed up on the back porch he wondered, as he had so many times since he had left, why Bert stayed here in partnership with a man he hated when there was no real reason for him to stay. But now Tom found no more reasonable answer than he'd ever had.

Rose called supper just as Arnie came in and they sat down, Cynthia beside Tom, smiling in satisfaction as if she had known all the time that he would come back for her. Five years had brought change to all of them—Bert a little grayer, Rose with crow's feet around her eyes, Arnie grown until he was a big boy for eleven, his body straining against the seams of his clothes—but it was Cynthia who had changed most of all.

She wasn't plain as Bonnie had once said she was. Her black hair was done up in curls, and her blue dress fitted her well, the bodice cut so that her trim breasts were shown off to the best advantage. Rose had done these things for her, giving her feminine companionship and advice that she had lacked from the day her mother had died.

But there was something else about Cynthia that made Tom uneasy, a shining happiness in her dark eyes for which, he suspected, he was responsible. He had intended all along to marry her, but now, sitting across from Rose, he was reminded of Bonnie and an unfamiliar uneasiness possessed him.

There was a moment of silent constraint, then Bert said, "I just got in and was washing up, Tom. That's why we're late with supper. Otherwise we'd have had everything eaten up slicker'n a whistle."

"There's more," Rose said a little sharply. "Don't give him the idea we're living from hand to mouth."

"No, we're not hard up," Bert admitted. "Arnie fetches in a rabbit or a sage hen. Once in a while I get an antelope, or I take a pasear into the mountains and bring in a buck."

"Plenty of Bar D beef around, isn't there?" Tom asked.

They didn't laugh as he expected them to. Arnie said, "Not any more there ain't. We had trouble with old Dugan about eating some of his steers."

A tight silence, then Rose said, "I keep looking at you, Tom, trying to see in you the boy Bert brought north from Winnemucca that time, but you just don't fit. Maybe it's that mustache."

"And he's bigger," Bert said. "How much do you weigh?"

"About two hundred," Tom said. "A little less now, I guess, eating prairie fare the way I have been."

"We'll fatten you up," Cynthia said. "Nobody stays the same, Rose. A boy becomes a man. Isn't that natural?"

Rose laughed. "Of course it is. I was just thinking how natural it was to call him Tommy. The first time I saw him, I mean. But Tommy wouldn't fit now."

Arnie had been fidgeting around. When he had a chance, he broke in, "Pa, tell him what you were doing in the desert."

"I went after a couple of horses that were stolen," Bert said. "That's all."

"Get 'em back?" Tom asked.

"Sure he did," Arnie said eagerly. "They're in the corral right now. Tell him about the horse thieves, pa."

"Nothing much to tell," Bert said. "One of 'em's dead, and I winged the other one. Last I saw he was busting the breeze getting out of there. I had the horses, so I let him go."

"Man hunter," Rose murmured. "That's my Bert."

"Well hell," Bert said defensively. "I had to do it if I wanted my horses back. No use going after Broncho Quinn."

Tom looked at Bert, not understanding him at all. This gray, spare man talked as lightly about killing a horse thief and wounding another as he might talk about hunting a coyote, yet he went on putting up with Mike Dugan year after year.

After supper Bert drifted out to the corral, Arnie back to his wood-chopping, and Cynthia had to step outside for a moment, leaving Tom alone with Rose. He did not lose the opportunity to ask, "Bonnie? What about her, Rose?"

"Married," Rose answered. "I guess I should have written to you about it. It turned out she wasn't pregnant. I knew she was using it as a threat aimed right at Mike's heart. It worked in one way. He had a heart attack after you left. He wouldn't go to a doctor and he still won't. He'll have another one and it'll kill him, I suppose."

"Who did Bonnie marry?"

"A middle-aged banker in San Francisco named Jared Evans. Mike sent both of us to San Francisco right after you left and put Bonnie in school. She ran away twice. When she got a chance to marry, she jumped at it."

"Is she happy?"

"No. Bonnie will never be happy. Not any more than Mike will. They're exactly alike. No matter what they have, they aren't satisfied. I did my best with Bonnie, but I failed."

"No you—"

"No excuses, Tom. I know Bonnie better than

149

anyone. I watched her change right under my eyes and I couldn't do a thing about it. After she got married, there wasn't anything else I could even try to do, so I came back and married Bert." She leaned forward, studying him. "I'm not sure I know you, Tom. Five years can do so much to a man. Funny, because I used to know you so well. It's just that you're older and more confident, and I . . . I'm afraid a little hard."

"I've been on my own," he said. "I bought and ran a ranch and I made money doing it. I even sold at a profit during hard times when some of my neighbors were going broke. I didn't make my money being soft."

She hesitated, then asked, "I'm prying, but I've got to know a couple of things. Are you going to marry Cynthia?"

He hesitated, not sure what the causes were that had made the urge to return to Indian Valley so inevitable. He had been given a good offer for his ranch and he had taken it and started out, but it hadn't been that simple. From the moment he had left Aunt Sadie in Cheyenne, he had known he would come back some day. The only question had been when.

"You can't go on dangling Cynthia," Rose said sharply. "She'll never love anyone else, but it's better—"

"I'm not going to keep her dangling," Tom said, his tone matching hers. "I'll marry her if she'll have me."

"She'll have you," Rose said. "This is the day she's been living for."

"What about Mike? Is he any better than he was?"

"He'll never be any better. I just hope you marry Cynthia and get out of the country."

"No, that's the one thing I can't do, even for Cynthia." She came in through the back door. He rose and went to her, and taking her hands, looked down at her. He said, "I came back to marry you if you'll have me, but—"

"Of course I'll have you," she said.

"Don't give me your answer yet," he said. "There's another thing. Rose thinks I ought to go somewhere else, but I've got to stay here. I can't tell you why. I'm not sure enough to even try to put it into words. I just know I've got to stay."

"I don't want to leave," she told him.

"Even knowing what Mike Dugan might do?"

"I'm not afraid," she said.

He glanced around and saw that Rose had left the room. He said, "Then I've got your answer. Set the date."

"Any time," she said. "My dress is already made. I've been sure you'd come and that you'd ask me. It had to be that way. It just had to."

He saw that there were tears in her eyes and that her lips were trembling. His feelings were beyond his understanding, for he remembered that Bonnie had said Cynthia loved him, and just now Rose had told him Cynthia would never love anyone else. She would be all a wife could be, a wife he would be proud of, the mother of his children. But he was uneasy. Things were moving too fast. Too many scores were waiting to be settled. This woman in his arms was a stranger. He wasn't sure he loved her in the way he had once thought he loved Bonnie.

He kissed her, stifling the doubt, and found her lips sweet and moist and eager. He asked, "When?"

"Pa will want to go to Prineville and get Pete," she said, "and you'll have to go to Starbuck and see if the preacher can come. We'll have it late Sunday afternoon. That will give him time to get here from town." She smiled slightly, and added, "It will be the right time of the moon for me, too."

Tom found that the preacher would be glad to come Sunday, even though it meant a hard ride after church. He was working for Mike Dugan, helping hay on Wineglass, and he couldn't spare the time on a weekday.

Pete rode in late Saturday. He had developed into the man he had promised to become five years ago, but he was still slim and tough as a piece of rawhide, and there was a boyish eagerness in his eyes when he shook hands.

"By God, I'm glad to see you," he said. "You should have come back sooner. Mike Dugan has lived too long."

Tom had often wondered if Pete and Cynthia knew about their mother. Now, seeing the brooding hatred in Pete's eyes, he decided that the boy did.

"I don't know what you're fixing to do," Pete went on, "but whatever it is, I'm throwing in with you.

Don't tell me I can't. I've quit my job, and I sure as hell won't stay here and work for pa."

"I'm not staying here, either," Tom said. "We'll figure it out."

"Good," Pete said.

The preacher arrived on time, his horse showing how hard he had ridden to get here when he did. He didn't waste a minute after he was in the house, letting them know he had to work the next day. The ceremony was a short and simple one, the preacher making the most of his moment of glory.

Tom kissed Cynthia as soon as they were pronounced man and wife, and drew back, feeling guilty because he saw a shining happiness in her eyes that she would not see in his. Again the doubts assailed him, for he had a terrifying feeling that Bonnie was here in this room, laughing at him and saying, "When you get into bed with her tonight, you'll think of me."

Then he heard Cynthia say softly, "I love you, Tom. I love you so much."

The preacher kissed Cynthia and shook hands with Tom, congratulating him. Bert and Pete did the same. Rose cried and kissed them both, and said, "I'm sorry, but I feel like a mother, and a mother always cries at her daughter's wedding."

Arnie, standing by the door, was staring at something that puzzled him. Then he let out a whoop that was not a proper sound for a wedding. He yelled excitedly, "Tom, get your gun. That damned Dugan's a-coming."

chapter 20

FOR A MOMENT no one spoke or even moved. Only Arnie seemed to be fully alive. He shouted, "Hurry up, Tom. He'll be here in a minute or two."

Bert said as if he were dazed, "He sent word the other day he wanted to see me, but he didn't say what about. I sure didn't think he'd come today."

"Of all days," Rose said bitterly.

"I'd best be going," the preacher said. "I've got to work tomorrow."

"Here." Tom handed him a ten-dollar gold piece. "Thanks for coming out."

"Glad to." The preacher grabbed the coin. "You got a pretty bride, Mr. Gordon. Real pretty." He went through the door on the run and struck off across the yard toward his horse.

"There goes a man who'll never see trouble," Pete said. "He won't let it catch up with him."

Tom had been trying to make a decision, feeling Cynthia's hand on his arm, sensing that her worried eyes were on his face. There was one important fact he didn't know. Had Dugan heard he was back? If Dugan did know, what were his intentions? Would he force a fight here in front of his sister and Cynthia?

Tom wheeled toward the antlers near the door where he had hung his gun belt, but Cynthia pulled at his arm, her face white. "No, Tom. Don't make a fight out of it. Not today."

Rose nodded. "Mike's not here for trouble. Don't force it."

"How do you know he's not here for trouble?" Tom demanded.

"He wouldn't have come alone."

He remembered what Todd Moody had said after the visit to Corrigan, that Dugan wasn't a man to gamble. Rose was right. Turning, Tom followed Bert outside into the hot afternoon sunshine, their long shadows moving beside them over the trodden dirt of the yard.

Pete came next, grumbling because Rose had not let him get his gun. The women were the last to leave the house. They stopped just outside the door, waiting, their anxious eyes on Dugan. Arnie, crazy with excitement, skipped back and forth in front of the house until Bert said sharply, "Stop it, Arnie," and jerked his head at the boy. Crestfallen, Arnie backed up against the wall beside Rose.

Dugan reined up in front of Bert, a faint smile on his lips. "Quite a reception committee." He touched his hat brim, bowing slightly in Cynthia's direction. "Afternoon, ma'am." Ignoring Rose, he brought his gaze back to Bert's face. "Did I interrupt something?"

"You did," Bert said. "Cynthia and Tom were just married."

"Congratulations, Cynthia." He gave her a bare, half-inch nod. "I hope you will be happy."

"Thank you, Mr. Dugan," Cynthia said.

As far as Dugan was concerned, Tom wasn't there, but he was convinced that Dugan's purpose in coming today was to show everyone here that Tom's presence meant nothing to him.

Dugan's gaze returned to Bert, but before he could say anything, Tom hit him with the words, "I'm here, Dugan. You can look over me and around me and beneath me, but I'll still be here."

"Why, so you are," Dugan said. "I hadn't seen you."

Tom knew he should have expected it just as he knew that a crazy show of anger on his part would make him appear small in front of everyone. He took a long breath, his eyes meeting Dugan's, and he felt the pressure of aroused temper, but he didn't give way to it. He held his silence until he knew he could say what he wanted to, refusing to permit the irritating, bland smile on Dugan's face to break his self-control.

"The last time we saw each other," Tom said, "you were going to use a knife on me. You told me to stay off this range, but I'm back and I aim to stay here. Now I'm asking your intentions. If you're figuring on making trouble for me, let's have it."

"Not on your wedding day," Dugan said, "but I will give you some advice. Take your bride and leave the country. If you do stay here, keep out of my way."

He turned his eyes to Bert again. Now the anger broke through Tom's self-restraint. In spite of his resolve to keep his temper, Tom raised his voice. "I'll stay here, Dugan, and I may not keep out of your way."

Dugan ignored it. He said, "Bert, I have business with you. What I have to say is private."

Bert shook his head. "Say what you have to say before my family. If you're breaking up our partnership, I want them to know why."

Dugan scowled. His gaze turned to Arnie who was digging a toe back and forth through the dust, then he swung his head to face Bert again. "All right, I'll tell you why I came. It wasn't to argue with this saddle tramp you let marry into your family. It's about the boy Arnie. As you know, I have only one child, Bonnie. She's married and lives in San Francisco. Bar D means nothing to her. I don't have any brothers or sisters."

Rose would have been better off to have remained silent, Tom thought, but she could not. Taking the bait, she cried out, "It's like Tom said, Mike. You can look over me and around me and beneath me, but I'm still here."

"Not in my will." Dugan's bland smile deepened as he nodded at Bert. "What I had in mind for Arnie was to have him live on the Bar D for, well, say a year. If we get along, he'll stay and I'll teach him the cattle business. My way, Bert, not yours. If he is capable of learning as I think he is, I'll make him my heir."

"No," Arnie screamed. "I won't go to live on your Goddamned old ranch."

"Arnie," Rose ordered. "Go inside."

The boy obeyed reluctantly. Dugan said, "Bert, you're too easy with him just like you are with everything. If he comes to me, I'll discipline him."

"He won't go to you," Bert said with quiet dignity.

157

"I've always treated him as my son. I'll go on treating him that way."

"And my adopted son," Rose added. "You've lost whatever chance you ever had for him, Mike."

"Then God have mercy on you when he grows up and finds out you kept him from inheriting a million dollars," Dugan said. "Now there is one more thing. I will not allow this fellow Gordon to live on any ranch which belongs to me. That includes the Lazy K."

"It's your ranch, but it's my home," Bert said, his voice shaking.

"I'll give you a week to vacate."

"Half the Lazy K cattle are mine. You can't just—"

"Meet me in Starbuck tomorrow morning at ten," Dugan said. "I'll settle up with you."

He wheeled his black and rode away. For a moment Bert's eyes met Rose's. He muttered, "Dugan's right. About Arnie when he grows up."

"We couldn't do anything else, Bert," she said.

"And another thing," he went on. "You don't have a home now."

"I'm glad," Rose said.

"It was overdue, Bert," Tom said. "Long overdue."

Pete, his anger bottled up in him until he was afraid to say anything, stomped off toward the shed. Rose put an arm around Cynthia. "I'll go cook your wedding supper. Don't let this spoil your day, dear."

Cynthia nodded, trying not to cry, but the tears came, and she whirled and ran into the house. Tom said, "You must hate him, Rose, even if he is your brother."

She looked at Bert, his face clearly reflecting the misery that was in him. "I'm glad we're leaving, Bert. You hear? Glad."

He nodded, but Tom, watching him, wasn't sure he did hear. Then she said to Tom, "Yes, I hate my brother. It's easy to hate him. He has no God but Mike Dugan. There is no defense against him. I had none in all the years I lived on the Bar D. Even his men, like Todd Moody and Lew Roman must hate him." She sighed, and turned toward the house, adding dully, "I'll get supper on the stove."

She said something to Arnie who came outside and wandered around aimlessly for a moment, kicked at a pile of dry horse manure to vent his anger, then saw Pete and crossed the yard to him.

Bert was staring at Dugan and his horse, little more than a dot across the sage, then Dugan dropped over the rim into Indian Valley and disappeared from sight. Tom said, "We'll buy a ranch together, Bert. I'll be a better partner than Dugan ever was."

"Sure you will," Bert said.

"How much will you get for your share of the Lazy K herd?"

"Maybe a couple thousand, beef prices low like they are. I've got $3,000 in the Starbuck bank. That's it, Tom. A lifetime of hard work and I'll walk out of here with not more'n $5,000 in my pocket."

"It's more'n some men have," Tom said. "What happened to Marvin Gentry?"

"He shot himself after Dugan took Wineglass over."

He paused and said with obvious effort, "I won't do that, Tom. By God, I won't do it because it's what he wants. You know, to my knowledge Dugan has never shot a man. He's never had to."

"What about Corrigan?"

"Died in Canyon City about a year after Dugan gave him that beating. He was never the same after Dugan got done with him."

"Eddie Vance?"

"He's in Prineville working on a newspaper. He just walked out, figuring the odds were too tough."

Tom rolled a smoke, pondering a question he had to ask. He was afraid of what it would do to Bert, but still he had to ask, and finally decided it would be good for Bert to face it. He said, his voice gentle, "Why have you stayed here so long, feeling the way you do about Dugan, and Rose feeling like she does?"

"You know," Bert said wearily. "I kept hoping his sins would catch up—"

"I know the answers you've always given," Tom broke in. "You've waited for the day of the reaper. He was Rose's brother. You didn't have any other place to go where you'd do as well as you did here. You had a family to raise. They were all excuses, Bert. Now what was the real reason?"

Bert rubbed his forehead as if trying to quiet the pounding ache that was there. Then he said with bitter self-condemnation, "I'm a coward, Tom. If he'd been any other man, I would have killed him as soon as I was sure he was Arnie's father, but not Mike Dugan."

Tom shook his head. "You're no coward, Bert. Ben Lampe wasn't a coward. Corrigan wasn't, and I don't want to believe I was for sitting my saddle and letting him take that beating."

"No, you weren't. I guess the truth is I don't really know why I've stayed. I never suspicioned about my wife and Dugan. I knew I wasn't making her happy. She wanted to leave here and I wouldn't go. Then she told me she was pregnant and she acted queer when she told me, but I still didn't guess what had happened. Arnie came along and I was surprised at the red hair, but the idea that Dugan could of got to her just never occurred to me. A few days later she told me and I said things I shouldn't have. I don't think she could have helped herself, but I didn't understand that then. A few days later we had a bad storm. She walked out into it. It was her way of committing suicide."

"All this time you've been blaming yourself," Tom said, "and you thought that shooting Dugan wouldn't help."

"I suppose that's it," Bert said. "I kept thinking I had to make up for failing my wife. Sort of a penance, I guess."

Tom laid a hand on his shoulder. "You're not to blame, Bert. You can't go on thinking that."

"I've never talked this way to anyone," Bert said, "except Rose. She told me the same."

"Want me to go with you tomorrow?"

"No." Then the misery and the torture of these last years caught up with Bert and he wheeled and

161

walked away, his shoulders shaking.

Worried, Tom called, "Bert? You all right, Bert?"

"I'm all right," he answered, his voice muffled. "Just let me alone."

Supper was a quiet meal, gloom shadowing all of them. Even Arnie, usually irrepressible, gulped his food and scooted outside again.

Later, standing beside Cynthia in her lean-to room, Tom glanced around, thinking how feminine it was and how much Rose had done for her. Her clothes hanging from a corner pole, the sweet smell of lavender that pervaded everything in the room, the pine bureau with its tatted doily and the Waterbury clock covered by red plush, a jewel box on top, the tiny thermometer to the left of the face, and the two slender perfume bottles on the right.

"I should have brought you a present," he said. "A wedding present. I never thought of it when I was in Starbuck."

She had started to unbutton her bodice. She dropped her hands to her side, staring at him in a way she never had before. "Yourself is enough," she said. "Tom, you've got to destroy him. He's a monster. He can't go on living."

She hated Dugan, too. He saw it mirrored in her face and then it was gone, and he was shocked. He had never imagined her capable of hating anyone, not the gentle Cynthia he had known as far back as the first Christmas he had spent here ten years ago.

She flushed, and going to him, put her arms around

him and laid her head against his chest. "I'm sorry. I didn't intend to say that."

"You know about your mother?"

"Of course I know. I've always known. But this isn't the time to talk about it. Blow out the lamp, darling. I want to undress in the dark."

After the pain of their first meeting had passed, she crept into his arms and lay against him. Then, her mouth close to his ear, she whispered, "I've loved you for so long, Tom. All the time you were gone I was afraid you'd meet someone else you liked."

He lay awake after she had gone to sleep on his arm, troubled by nagging doubts he could not silence.

chapter 21

BERT LEFT BEFORE SUNUP the next morning so he would reach Starbuck in time for his date with Dugan, but before he rode off, Tom joined him at the corral. He said, "Pete'n me are taking a pasear over the north half of the valley and back into the mountains. You know of any outfit that's for sale?"

"No." Bert stepped into the saddle. "I don't get into that country very often."

"We may be gone two, three days," Tom said. "I'm either going to buy a ranch, or I'll find a likely place where I can file on a quarter section and start from scratch. I'd like to have you for a partner, but since you won't be able to go with me, I've got to pick out the place. You may not like it."

"I'll like it," Bert said.

"What I mean is, you'll have enough cash money to start a town business or buy a ranch a hundred miles from here. You don't have to throw in with me just because—"

"You trying to get out of something, Tom?"

"Hell no. I just didn't want you to feel you were bound to anything on my account. Or Cynthia's. I thought after you figured on it a spell, you and Rose might want to take Arnie and get to hell out of the country."

Bert leaned forward to stare at Tom in the opalescent dawn light. Tom could not see his face clearly, but it seemed to Tom that it was more gray than ever. He was, Tom suspected, actually afraid in a physical way of meeting Dugan today, but he was bound to do it.

"It don't make any difference what Rose and me want," Bert said. "I can't leave this country any more'n you can. You go ahead and pick out the spread you'n Pete and Cynthia will like. It'll be all right with me'n Rose and Arnie."

He rode off, angling northeast toward the rim. Watching him, Tom thought that neither of them was a free man. But no man was free, when it came to that. Even Mike Dugan was cast in a rigid mold so that he would never be free of his own greed and ambition and vindictiveness. Everyone, or so it seemed, and now Tom knew it included Cynthia, wanted to see Dugan destroyed, but the question was how. The answer might be a long time coming.

A few minutes later Tom and Pete struck off to the northwest, Tom having apologized to Cynthia for leaving so soon. "Someday we'll have a honeymoon," he said, and she kissed him and said, smiling, "Someday I'll make you keep that promise."

When Tom had been on the Bar D, he had become familiar with the country south of the lakes and north as far as Starbuck. Actually he knew very little about the rest of the valley except that the land east of Duck River was rocky, much of it covered with greasewood instead of sage, and that, he knew, was a bad sign. He should have asked Bert's advice, but it was too late now, so he turned to Pete.

"Right down there around Indian Lake is where I'd start looking," Pete said in answer to Tom's question. "Sure it's inside Dugan's fence, but he don't own the marginal land around the lake. Folks are going to settle down there and Dugan's gun guards that ride his fence every day won't keep 'em out."

"I don't savvy what you mean by marginal land," Tom said.

"The land around the lake. It's gone down a lot since you left. Dugan's got a crew of men clearing off the tules and making hay meadows out of land that used to be under water, but that don't give him legal title to it. Sure, he's got title to his land on the Frying Pan, but how'n hell could he own land that wasn't land when he did the buying?"

He considered what Pete said, knowing that the so-called "marginal land" would be sub-irrigated from the lake and would produce three tons of hay to the acre, whereas the bench land he wanted wouldn't average more than a third of that. On the other hand, to move inside Dugan's fence would bring on an immediate clash regardless of the legal rights involved, and Tom wasn't ready for it.

So he said, "A good idea, but I guess I want a few pine trees around me. We'll start east of Hampton Buttes and see what we can find."

"By God, you're as scared of Dugan as the old man is," Pete said harshly. "I didn't think you would be."

"If you think I'm scared," Tom said, "you'd better light out for Crooked River and get your old job back."

"Maybe I had," Pete said furiously. He was evidently as hot-tempered as ever. "I figure you had enough guts to make a fight, but I was sure dreaming."

"There's a right time and a wrong time to do things," Tom said. "I'll know the right time when it comes. There's another thing you ought to think about. The last four, five years have been dry, haven't they?"

"Yes, but—"

"All right. There'll be wet years coming. When they do, the lake will be as big as it used to be, and then where'll your marginal land be?"

Pete's face turned red. "Under water, I guess. Hell, I never thought of that."

"Still want to head back to Crooked River?"

"No," Pete said. "I'll string along. You're smarter'n I am. I might as well admit it."

They searched for three days, spending the first

166

night in the mountains with an old man named Barney Dukes who had filed on a meadow with a spring and ran a few head of cattle.

"It's the timber I was looking for," Dukes told Tom. "I got the best stand of pine on this side of the divide. Someday a railroad's coming into this country. Then there'll be sawmills, and I'll get rich off my timber."

On the way down Duck River the next day, Tom said, "The old man's right. Trouble is, he won't live to see it."

Pete laughed. "A crazy old coot if I ever seen one. You'n me will be old men before Indian Valley sees a railroad."

Most of the outfits they saw on the second day were ten-cow spreads with poor buildings and not enough hay land, a vital deficiency in the mountains where winters were severe. The people, it seemed to Tom, were as poverty-stricken as the dry-land farmers east of Duck River.

That night they stayed at the Diamond A on Moon Creek, which flowed into Duck River from the west. It was two miles from Eula, about four from Starbuck, and belonged to a man named Alex Grimes, who had been in the country almost as long as Mike Dugan.

Tom remembered seeing Grimes in Starbuck when he'd been on the Bar D, a mountain of a man who was too fat to work, but had a family of sons who rode for him. Everything about the ranch showed that Grimes was prosperous, so Tom never even asked him if he wanted to sell.

He did mention Barney Dukes, and Grimes said, "Don't go to thinking he's crazy. A railroad's coming sure as the sun's gonna rise in the morning. Mike Dugan knows it. He's been moving north right along. And why? He wants everbody to think he's out to steal grass, but the truth is he's got his eyes on the timber. In another ten years he'll control the Duck River watershed clean to the divide."

"What'll happen to you?" Tom asked.

Grimes swore. "You know without asking. He's got my tail in a crack now." Grimes jabbed a fat forefinger at Tom. "But there's one thing that'll save us. The hard times in the East and Middle West will bring more settlers in. Remember the Kansas Sufferers who were coming in when you were here?"

Tom nodded, and Grimes went on, "Most of 'em starved out and moved on. A few are hanging tight. I helped some of 'em, but with the price of beef down like it is, I've got all I can do to help myself. Now we're gonna get a new bunch, and I figure we'll be able to outvote Dugan's buckaroos and them in town that suck after him all the time."

"What good's that going to do?" Tom asked.

"We'll put in a new bunch of county officials, that's what," Grimes said. "We might even move the county seat to Eula. Dugan's closed the county road up the Frying Pan. That's how he got me over a barrel. If I want to get my beef to the railroad, I've got to let him do the driving and shipping out of Winnemucca, but if we force that road open, we've got him where the hair's short."

168

Tom shook his head. "I didn't see much at Eula that looked like a county seat."

"You will." Grimes laughed shortly. "Not much there now, but I'm betting my blue chip on Andrew Hamilton. He hates Dugan, and he's not afraid to buck him. Maybe he's a dreamer, but he's no wilder'n Mike Dugan was twenty years ago when he settled on the Frying Pan. Hamilton's building a schoolhouse and he'll have a teacher on hand, come fall. I fetched in a blacksmith for him from Canyon City the other day. I've tried to get Eddie Vance to come back from Prineville, but he won't do it. He used to like you. Maybe you can change his mind."

"I'll try," Tom said, "if I can find a ranch to buy."

"Come morning," Grimes said, "you ride up Moon Creek to the Rafter T. It's 'bout four miles above here. Belongs to Harley Bangs. He lost his wife and now his pa's laid up with a broken leg. He can't afford to hire help, and he can't work it himself."

"How much of a herd has he got?"

"Book counts 400 head. It ain't off much, either. Most of it she stuff. He had a good calf crop. I'd say he's got 40, maybe 50 head of steers to go this fall."

"What does Bangs want for the outfit?"

Grimes squinted at Tom, his faded blue eyes almost lost behind layers of fat. "Depends on what you've got." He paused, but Tom didn't enlighten him. "Well, Harley's asking $12,000. He'll take less. But if you ain't got it, don't buy. It's the Goddamned interest that eats a man up and makes Russ Ordway rich. Dugan, too."

"I don't have $12,000."

Grimes showed his disappointment. "I hoped you had. I need a tough neighbor. Harry Winch, he's got the Cross 9 just up the creek, he's softer'n mush unless I keep pushing him."

"How much land has Bangs got title to?"

"Half a section. It's all hay land. There's plenty of water. Summer graze in the mountains to the north, winter graze in the valley to the south. House sets down in a dip so it's kind o' out o' the wind. Wish I could afford to buy it, but I ain't gonna let Ordway get his hooks into me."

Tom slept in the bunkhouse that night. He thought about the Rafter T before he went to sleep and again when he woke at dawn. If Grimes had told it straight, the Rafter T was the spread he wanted. If the book count was right, the $12,000 wasn't far off, even at the present low price of beef. But it would take most of the cash he and Bert had.

All the talk about a railroad coming and about outvoting Dugan and changing the county seat was dream talk. If a man had to throw his steers in with the Bar D drive and take what he could get, he was whipped. All Dugan had to do was to refuse to take Tom's cattle for a couple of years and he was up a tree.

But the instant he looked at the Rafter T the next morning, he knew he had to have it, gamble or not. It was almost as if the ranch had been created to fill the dream he'd had. Plenty of water coming down Moon Creek even in a dry summer. Tight buildings. Corrals that had been kept in good repair. A few pine trees around the house. And all the deeded land was along the creek and could be irrigated with a little work on the ditch.

Harley Bangs was a worried man. He had about half his hay up, but he said, "If I stay here, I dunno how I'll get through the winter. Pa," he pointed at the old man sitting in a rocking chair on the porch, "he can't do no work. Busted a leg last spring and it ain't never healed right."

"Grimes said you wanted $12,000," Tom said. "That's way high, times being what they are. Maybe you'd take $1,000 down and a mortgage for the balance?"

Bangs looked at him as if he thought Tom was crazy. "I've got to take Pa to the Willamette Valley where the winters ain't as tough as they are here. What could I buy for $1,000?"

"You'd have the mortgage for $11,000."

"I couldn't turn it to Ordway for half that." Bangs shook his head. "I'm in bad shape, but not that bad."

"It's a good spread, Tom," Pete said. "Better raise the ante."

Tom shook his head. "I don't know how many cows you've got, Bangs. I don't have time to comb the hills to see if you've got 400 head."

"I know the count's right," Bangs said stubbornly. "I'll guarantee it within 10 percent."

"If you'll guarantee your count, I'll give you $9,000 cash," Tom said. "Cash, that is, except for $1,000

171

which I'll hang onto till fall to see if your guarantee's any good."

Bangs cried out as if he were in physical pain. "That's three-quarters of what the outfit's worth."

"Take it or leave it," Tom said, "but before you leave it, you'd better ask yourself where you'll look to find that much cash." He tapped his chest. "I've got it, mister."

Tom walked to his horse and mounted. He moved slowly, giving Bangs plenty of time to change his mind. He had a bad thirty seconds because he knew he could not let this outfit get away from him. He remembered bargaining with Aunt Sadie. He'd won with her, but this time he was afraid he'd lost.

He started to ride off before Bangs called angrily, "I'll take it. You're a damned robber, but I'll take it."

"I'll see you in Starbuck at noon tomorrow," Tom said, and kept on riding.

"That was close," Pete said when he caught up with Tom. "I figured you'd made a mistake."

Tom turned his head to wink. He said, "I'll tell you something, Pete. I did, too."

chapter 22

THE NEWS OF THE PURCHASE of the Rafter T was well received that night. Arnie was tickled because there were fish in Moon Creek, and being close to the timber, he could go deer hunting every day. Cynthia and Rose were glad they had a place to move to.

They'd start packing in the morning.

But it was Bert's reaction that particularly pleased Tom. "You bought one of the best outfits in the valley," Bert said. "I would have mentioned it to you, but I hadn't heard Harley Bangs wanted to sell. He's a careful man, Harley is, and it's my guess you won't find his book count off very much."

"You'll go to town with me tomorrow?" Tom asked.

Bert nodded, his face expressionless. "I'll go."

Bert said nothing that evening about his settlement with Dugan. He didn't mention it on the way to Starbuck the following morning, either. Tom was curious, but he hesitated to ask. As they rode through Eula, Tom noticed that two new buildings had been started, a blacksmith shop near the store, and the schoolhouse across the street.

Bert waved to a man who was working on the schoolhouse. He said, "That's Andrew Hamilton."

"Arnie ever been to school?" Tom asked.

"No," Bert said. "We've taught him at home."

"He needs schooling," Tom said. Bert, not wanting to argue, remained silent. Tom told him what Alex Grimes had said about Eula, adding, "I'll have some money left over after we settle with Bangs. I've got a notion to pick up some of Hamilton's lots."

Bert shook his head. "A waste of money. Starbuck's the county seat and Dugan will see it stays there. That's what makes a town. A year from now cows will be eating grass on Eula's Main Street."

"So Dugan goes right on running things the way he

has been," Tom said. "Closing county roads and paying half the taxes he should and picking the county officials."

"That's the way I figure it," Bert said bitterly. "A man can learn to live with a skunk under the house if he's a mind to."

"But he'll never get used to the smell," Tom said.

Bert said nothing to that, and they lapsed into silence as they crossed the river and rode into Starbuck. Bert was a beaten man, Tom thought. He had been ground into the dust. Something must have happened when he had settled up with Dugan.

They tied in front of the bank and went in. Harley Bangs was waiting for them. Russ Ordway took care of the paper work and watched the exchange of money with greedy eyes. He said the bank would be glad to keep the money for Bangs, but Bangs said no, he and his father would be leaving in three days. Tom and Bert could take possession then. He shook hands all around, refused Tom's offer of a drink to celebrate the sale, and rode out of town.

But Ordway was never one to turn down free whisky. He accompanied Tom and Bert to the Red Bull Saloon and drank to the successful operation of the Rafter T. Then he invited Bert and Tom to deposit their surplus cash in his bank.

"I don't aim to do business with any Dugan outfit," Tom said. "I guess you won't deny that your bank is a Dugan interprise."

"No," Ordway said, "but I'll tell you one thing,

Gordon. You won't do any business in this county if you don't patronize Dugan enterprises."

"I will," Tom said. "Starbuck's a dying town. In another year Eula will be the county seat."

Ordway looked at him as if he were out of his mind. "What are you talking about, man? There's nothing at Eula."

"There will be," Tom said.

"If you persist in operating along the lines you mention," Ordway said angrily, "you'll be busted in a year. You won't ship a single Rafter T steer out of Winnemucca." He ran the tip of his tongue over dry lips. "You won't only be busted, mister. You'll be dead."

Tom laughed as he watched Ordway slam out through the batwings. "He's worried or he wouldn't have got so mad."

"He's mad, but he's not worried." Bert stared gloomily at the amber liquid in his glass. "And I'm not worried about having a bank to put my money in. All I've got is a little loose change in my pocket."

"I don't savvy," Tom said. "You had $3,000, and you had $2,000 coming in your settlement with Dugan. That figures—"

"I got $1,500, not $2,000. I won't have enough to buy salt for the venison if I'm lucky enough to keep venison on the table."

"Oh hell, we'll eat at the same table. But I don't savvy. You said you—"

"You don't need to remind me what I said. It's just that when you get down to cases and you've got a pound coming but you can only get an ounce, then you'd better take the ounce." Bert picked up his glass and finished his drink. He said, "I'm going home. You come when you feel like it."

Tom watched him walk out, knowing he preferred to ride alone. He knew now what had happened. Dugan had cheated Bert and Bert had accepted it rather than fight. Dugan had not been satisfied until he had given the screw its last, torturing turn. But why?

Several possible answers occurred to Tom. Perhaps some strange quirk in Dugan made him regret what he had done to Bert's wife and he was reminded of it whenever he saw Bert. Or it could be that he was sore because Rose had left the Bar D and married Bert. Or, and this made the most sense, he was unable for the time being to get at Tom, but he could strike at Bert, and this was his way of telling Tom that he'd better leave the country.

Tom stopped in Eula on his way back to the Lazy K and bought three lots. He said to Hamilton, "I've had a talk with Alex Grimes. He thinks Eula will grow."

"Sure it will." Hamilton cocked his head to one side. "What have you got in mind for the lots you just bought?"

"Nothing in particular. Let's say it's an investment."

Hamilton shrugged. "Makes me no never mind. We've got a long ways to go, but the future looks pretty good to me."

"Not unless you get the county seat."

Hamilton scowled. "That's the tough one. We've got

176

enough votes in the county to win, I think, if we can get them out. Dugan just has his crew and a few ranchers who depend on him like Jim Becker on Mule Ear."

"There's the Starbuck votes," Tom reminded him, "and Sam Bell's Arrow."

Hamilton nodded. "I still say we've got enough votes. A lot of families scattered back in the hills and on the other side of Duck River. But it's foolish to risk an election until we're sure we can win, and we can't win until we get the facts into the people's minds. To do that we need a newspaper."

"If I find a good man with a printing press, will you put up a building for him?"

"You're damned right I will," Hamilton said. "I'll do better. I'll pay your man $50 a month. He's got to live and he won't make anything out of his paper for a while. What we've got to do is get a newspaper into the hands of every voter in the county."

"I'll see what I can do," Tom said.

The next day he tried to help Cynthia and Rose pack, but he decided he was in the way, so he quit and watched. Bert had taken Arnie and Pete and gone into the desert to round up the horses.

"We'll need them on the Rafter T," he told Tom. "You didn't make a deal for Bangs's horses, did you?"

"Just the cattle," Tom said.

"That's what I figured. Well, we'll fetch in all we can find. They're mine, and by God, Dugan had better not try to take them away from me."

177

He'd crumble just as he had on the money, Tom thought, if Dugan put the squeeze on him again, but maybe they'd have the horses off Lazy K range before Dugan knew what was happening. He thought about Eddie Vance as he watched the women pack, wondering what he could say to the man that would persuade him to come back to Indian Valley.

Cynthia worked at the packing with a hysterical frenzy that wore her out so that she had to go to her room and lie down in the middle of the afternoon. Rose took it more slowly, and when Cynthia left them, Rose decided she'd have a cup of coffee and that would be all the rest she needed.

"Cynthia has hated the Lazy K ever since her mother died," Rose said as she sat with Tom. "You're doing a good thing for her just by taking her away." She stirred her coffee thoughtfully, staring at it. "You know, Tom, it hasn't been easy, living here. Seems that there's a part of Bert that belongs to his first wife. I can't whip a ghost."

"Maybe moving will help," Tom said.

She nodded. "I'm hoping it will. If I could have come to him with a little money, it might have been different, but Mike was always tight with me. After Bonnie got married, I had enough to pay my boat passage from San Francisco to Portland, and up the Columbia to The Dalles, then by stage to Prineville and Starbuck. When I got here, I only had three silver dollars."

Rose finished her coffee and placed her hands on the

table and stared at them. They showed age more than her face, thin hands with liver spots on the backs, the knuckles swollen.

"I think Cynthia's mother came from a fairly well-to-do family," Rose said. "At least she never had to work very hard until she married Bert. The nice things that are in the house were hers; that Waterbury clock in Cynthia's room and the Ironstone plates we're packing so carefully, and the lamp with the hand-painted shade."

She nodded at the lamp which hung from the ceiling, the white shade gaily decorated with red flowers and green leaves. "Well, they're sacred because they belonged to Bert's wife. I guess they're part of the ghost and I'm afraid she'll move with us."

She brought the coffee pot and filled the cups, took the pot back to the stove and returned to sit beside him again. "Mike can't stand having anyone leave him. His wife did and he never got over it. He made it plain to me that I had a home on the Bar D as long as I wanted it, but if I left him, or left Bonnie after he sent her to San Francisco, he was finished with me. That's why he said when he was here that he had no sister. God, he's got a lot to answer for."

"He'll answer for it," Tom said.

She looked at him. "You're the only man who ever got through his hide. You held a gun on him and you'd have killed him and he knew it. You walked out of the house without him laying a hand on you. You made him lose Bonnie and me. He'll never forgive you.

Don't be fooled by his telling you to stay out of his way."

"I'm not."

"Don't be fooled by his waiting, either. On something like this he's got a wonderful lot of patience. You'd think a man of his nature couldn't wait to get at someone he hates, but his capacity for waiting is endless."

"So's mine."

"Yes, I guess it is." She smiled briefly. "I keep wondering if he'll write to Bonnie that you're here. She'll take the first train for Winnemucca the minute she hears."

He stirred uncomfortably. "She's forgotten me by now."

"No, she'll never forget you. Well, I've got to get back to work." She rose, leaving her cup of coffee on the table.

He left the next morning for Prineville, and that night found Eddie Vance drinking his supper in the hotel bar. Five years had not changed him, still tall and skinny with his gray eyes as bleary as they had been the last time Tom had seen him in Starbuck. He pretended he was too drunk to recognize Tom, but he couldn't make himself play the part to the end. Tom got him into a restaurant and ordered black coffee, steaming hot.

After two cups, Vance gave up. "You're a persistent son of a bitch," he grumbled. "I knew you'd be back the minute you left me that night in Starbuck, and why

I didn't get a thousand miles from here I don't know. But I'll tell you right now that whatever you want me to do is something I won't do."

But in his room with his pipe filled and going, Vance listened to Tom as he told what he'd done after he'd left the country, and about buying the Rafter T, and Eula and Andrew Hamilton's plans. He ended with, "I think if we work together, we can clean Dugan's plow for him."

"I'm not going back to Indian Valley."

"He promised he'd put up a building for you," Tom went on. "He'll subsidize you to the tune of $50 a month. I'll do the same for six months. You can't lose, Eddie."

"Nothing but my life," Vance said. "I told you I wasn't going back."

"Why did you leave?"

"I saw what happened to Corrigan. There were others like him about the same time. And I saw them."

"I don't figure that's all."

"There was a little more," Vance admitted. "I kind of rode the fence for a while, hating myself all the time. Then after you pulled your freight, I got it off my chest by firing both barrels in an editorial on the front page. I called him a monopolist and told everybody what the county government was. He waited three days and then he walked into my shop and laid the paper down in front of me and said he wanted a retraction and an apology in the next issue. Well, there wasn't any next issue. That's why I'm not going back."

"You said you wanted to be there when I got back. All right, I'm here. What are you going to do about it?"

"Not a damned thing. I wish you'd have stayed in Colorado."

"Because you don't like what your conscience is saying?"

Vance got up and, walking to the bureau, took a bottle out of the top drawer, stared at it, and put it back. He wheeled to face Tom. "I don't have a conscience. I'm a newspaper man. To hell with you and Indian Valley and Starbuck."

Tom rolled a cigarette, taking his time. He sealed it and held a match flame to it, then said, "Remember that Saturday in the Red Bull? Lew Roman was getting drunk and I said he didn't used to drink that way, and you said he had to. He had to forget old ambitions, old dreams, the right to call himself a man. You said—"

"Get out of here," Vance yelled. "By God, I remember what I said."

"Is that why you're drinking?" Tom pointed at the bottle.

"That's right. I left the right to call myself a man back there in Starbuck."

"I did, too," Tom said. "That's the real reason I came back. That's the reason Bert stayed around all this time. It's there for you, too, but you've got to go back and get it. This time you won't be alone. Andrew Hamilton's there. Alex Grimes is there. I'm there. Work with us to move the county seat to Eula. That's all I'm asking."

182

"All? That's a hell of a lot, mister."

"Is it too much for the right to call yourself a man again?"

Vance stared at Tom, blinking, then he whirled and picked up the whisky bottle and tossed it through the window. When the tinkle of falling glass had stopped, he said, "Tell your damned Hamilton to put up a building."

He kept his word. The first issue of the *Starbuck Weekly Herald* to be printed in Eula was in the mail the tenth of September. Two weeks later Andrew Hamilton had a post office, and that was Eddie Vance's first big story.

chapter 23

FROM THE DAY HE MOVED onto the Rafter T, Tom was caught up in a whirlwind of work that gave him no rest even on Sundays. He felt like a man who had fallen into a river in flood time and was being hurled end over end as he was carried downstream.

At first it was even worse for the women because the house was, as Rose put it mildly, "a boar's nest." For the first week everyone slept outside, Rose and Cynthia even cooking over an open fire. Arnie was kept busy carrying water from the creek and cutting wood to keep the fire going so the water would heat for the women's scrubbing.

There were two bedrooms in the house. Cynthia and Tom slept in one, Rose and Bert in the other, and Pete and Arnie slept in the bunkhouse. Once the house was clean, the pressure was off the women.

The bunkhouse was next, but it wasn't the problem the house had been because it hadn't been occupied recently, so there the work was swamping out an accumulation of dust and cobwebs that had gathered through months of nonuse. The house was different. The dirt was the dirty-dirt that came from human occupancy: grease in the kitchen, ashes and tobacco spit on the floor in the front room, and urine and vomit in the bedroom where the old man had slept.

Cutting and stacking hay was the immediate job for the men. Bangs had been far behind, having started too late. Tom and Bert took care of the haying, and Pete hauled manure out of the sheds and corrals. They were in the worst shape Tom had ever seen on any ranch, but he was thankful for one thing. Pete was a hard worker.

"I'm glad you're not one of these buckaroos like Todd Moody," Tom told Pete one evening. "He figures anything except riding a horse and looking at a cow's behind is beneath him."

"One thing about pa," Pete said, grinning a little. "He never spoiled me that way. When you grow up on a greasy-sack spread like the Lazy K, you learn that nothing's beneath you that has to be done."

"I can't ask your dad to spell you off," Tom said. "He's a better man stacking hay than either of us, and his back's bothering him, but I'll switch off with you."

Pete shook his head. "I told you I'd do it and I will.

Then I'll haul a few loads of gravel so them corrals won't mire a snipe next spring. I was exploring the other evening and found a pretty fair gravel bed up the creek a piece. After I get the gravel hauled, we've got to work on the fences."

"I know it," Tom said. "Especially around the horse pasture. That fence is sure shot to hell."

"Then we start cutting wood," Pete said with a groan. "Cut it and haul it down here so Arnie can get at it with his bucksaw. Sometimes I wonder why I ever left Crooked River."

Tom looked at him closely in the dusk light. "You mean that, Pete?"

"Hell no," Pete said. "I was just joshing, figuring that you sometimes wonder why you left Colorado."

"Well, I keep thinking we'll get caught up," Tom said, "and then we'll be able to take it a little easier."

"Sure we will," Pete said. "I'm not kicking. This is what me'n Cynthia always wanted. We used to talk about it clear back to the first time you spent Christmas with us. Seemed like the three of us belonged together." He flipped his cigarette stub into the yard. "We had a good time then, riding across the desert or playing a game after supper, and pa sitting by the stove with Arnie on his lap telling his crazy yarns about some poker game in Winnemucca or shooting somebody."

"Those yarns were true," Tom said. "Ben Lampe told me the same things about Bert."

Pete was silent for a minute, then he said, "I sure

185

wouldn't call you a liar, Tom, so I'll just call Ben Lampe one."

Tom let it go, knowing that no amount of argument would change Pete's opinion of his father that was based on Bert's failure to stand up to Mike Dugan.

"Funny about when you're kids," Pete went on in a brooding tone. "You have a hell of a lot of fun because you don't worry about things. I guess we worried, all right, but what I mean is you don't really understand things. Cynthia knew about ma and Dugan before I did, but she never told me. Pa didn't either. I guess it just kinda seeped in after a while. Then I kept thinking pa would take care of Dugan, but he never did, and now I know he never will, so I've got to. I don't know how much longer I can wait, Tom."

"You'll wait just like I'm waiting," Tom said. "We'll know when the time comes."

Pete swore. "Sure, you can wait. He didn't do to your mother what he done to mine."

"No, but he did something else," Tom said. He had never told Pete about Ben Lampe and Dora Lind, but he told him then, and added, "They weren't my parents, but they were special people to me. They gave me help when I needed it and I don't know what would have happened to me if they hadn't. Dugan killed Ben Lampe the way I look at it, and he ruined Dora Lind, but shooting Dugan isn't the answer."

"Then what the hell is the answer?"

"I don't know, only I tell you we'll know it when the time's right. Call it a hunch, but I'm as sure of it as I

186

can be sure of anything." He paused, his thoughts tracking back to what Pete had said about the three of them when they were kids. He had known Cynthia and Pete had been close, closer than most brothers and sisters, but now he realized they had been even closer than he had thought, and he asked, "Pete, is Cynthia happy?" Then, when the words were out and it was too late, he knew he shouldn't have said them.

Pete didn't answer for a moment, then he said, "Hell, I don't know. I guess she is. She always wanted to marry you. But she's like me about Dugan, only more so."

Without another word Pete got up and walked across the yard to the bunkhouse; Tom sat there a long time smoking one cigarette after another. Marriage was not what he had dreamed it would be. Maybe it was the hard work they had faced from the first day they had come here to the Rafter T, or maybe he hadn't started right with her. She never refused him except on the days of the month when she couldn't have him, but she didn't seem to enjoy it, either. She submitted, as if it were her duty. With many men that would have been enough, but not with Tom.

He hadn't been a puritan by any standard. When he'd lived in Colorado, he'd gone to the sporting houses in Denver when he'd made trips there for business reasons, and he'd gone to some in the mining camps of the San Juan above his ranch where business operated twenty-four hours a day and life in the towns too often seemed to be one wild debauch after another.

Some of the prostitutes were crude, some even were vicious women who would take a man for everything they could; there were others he felt sorry for because they had got into the wrong business and couldn't get out, but in no case did he find any real satisfaction. His physical congestion was relieved. Beyond that there was nothing.

He knew there was more to having a woman than the cold-blooded, commercial service the prostitutes performed. He had tasted it once on the shoulder of North Medicine Peak with Bonnie. He had expected to find the same hunger and desire in Cynthia he had found in Bonnie, and he wasn't sure why he hadn't.

Cynthia loved him. Or maybe he was wrong about her. Maybe she just looked to him to destroy Dugan the way everyone else seemed to. He turned it over in his mind, but he couldn't figure it through. He finally gave up thinking about it and ground out his cigarette stub.

He went to bed, undressing in the dark, and slipped in beside Cynthia. She said drowsily, "I thought you were never coming to bed."

She slid over on his arm and, with her mouth close to his ear, she said, "Tom, I've got something to tell you. I've been wanting to tell you, but I never could get around to it. You're going to be a father."

His heart began skipping every other beat. He had thought about this, of course, confident it would happen, but hoping it would be postponed. He wasn't ready for a baby and he didn't think she was. A few more months, time to make the adjustments that every marriage took. . . .

She slid off his arm and turned over, giving him her back, and he knew at once he had made a mistake, a serious one. This was no time for regret, it was a time to be happy and he should have said so.

He took hold of her and forced her around so that she faced him. "I'm glad," he said. "I was just surprised. Funny what a man thinks of when he hears a thing like that. You want me to tell you what I thought?"

Her face was buried against his chest so that her "yes" was muffled and barely reached his ears.

"I was thinking that all of our work getting started here won't be wasted. I was seeing myself the age of your dad with our kids around us, and I felt good, knowing they were getting one of the best ranches in Indian Valley."

She began to cry, and he forced her face away from him so he could kiss her. He said, "Hey now, this is no time to be crying."

"I know," she said. "It's silly. I'm happy. I wanted you to be glad, Tom. I wanted it so much, and I was afraid you weren't."

"Sure I'm glad," he said, and kissed her again, hating himself for lying.

The next day Todd Moody rode up the creek from Harry Winch's Cross 9 just as Tom and Bert came in from the hay field. He sat his saddle in front of the house, a saddle almost as fine as Dugan's, and grinned at Tom who walked toward him, leaving Bert to unhook and take care of the horses.

"Howdy, Tommy," Todd said affably, smiling. "Heard you were back."

Todd had changed, changed more than anyone else Tom had seen since he'd returned. It wasn't the way he sat his horse, easy and balanced, or the expensive saddle and pearl-handled gun on his hip, or his clothes, which were expensive, from the Stetson which he wore at a rakish angle on down to his hand-tooled boots. Not even the smile which was as false as a horse trader's claims for the animal he was trying to sell.

Rather, it was a sense of power that was stamped upon him, of brutality, of a conviction that anything Bar D did was right. He was, as Tom had once thought, a young Lew Roman, but tougher and meaner, without Roman's weakness for drink. Then Tom told himself he wasn't really seeing those things in Todd's face, but rather he had been so sure that was the Todd Moody he'd see.

"Forget how to talk, Tommy boy?" Todd asked. "Hell man, you used to run on like a magpie."

"I can still talk," Tom said. "I was wondering what brought you here. You're Bar D and I'm Rafter T, and we don't have a damned thing to do with each other."

"We will, son, we will," Todd said, laughing. "That's why I'm here. You've got some chuckle-headed ideas about cutting Mike down to size. You're whipped, Tommy boy, and you'll be crawling out of the valley on your belly. Try going to Sylvester Chase to see if you can buy supplies. Or to Russ Ordway and see if you can borrow money."

Todd tapped himself on the chest. "Come to me and see if Bar D will trail your steers to the railroad like we'll take Cross 9's and Diamond A's. I'm rodding the outfit now and I'll tell you something, son. You're broke."

He laughed, then turned his horse and rode back down the creek. He hadn't even given Tom a chance to say he'd never let a Rafter T steer go with a Bar D drive no matter how bad off he was. He had expected trouble, even a raid, but nothing had happened. Now he realized he had been foolish to expect it. This was Dugan's way, and Todd had simply come to brag, confident that his aces would haul in the pot any day in the year.

They had finished the work except for the wood-hauling by the time fall roundup started, but the day before they were ready to start Bert's back gave out on him. He went to bed, finding it hard to even lie flat on his back. He couldn't turn himself, and he cried out in agony when anyone else turned him. Tom sent Pete to Starbuck for Doc Sims, but there wasn't much the doctor could do.

"Put some heat on his back where it hurts," Sims said. "You know, hot irons wrapped so they won't burn. Might give him some relief, but this is something he'll just have to wear out."

Tom had him examine Cynthia and he pronounced

her as strong and healthy as a young mare and said she'd have her baby without trouble. Then, as he walked to his buggy with Tom, he said, "I'm worried about Bert. He's an old man, and I don't mean that in terms of time. You'll have to get him off the ranch. It's my opinion he'll never be able to do a day's work."

Sims was a little man with a goat-like beard and sparrow eyes, and he moved like a bird, but he was a good doctor and Tom had no reason to mistrust him. Still, he did, simply because Sims had moved to Starbuck years ago when Sylvester Chase and Russ Ordway had come.

Tom waited until Sims picked up the metal weight, deposited it in the buggy, and stepped into the seat. Then he said, "Doc, Mike Dugan owns just about everything in Starbuck, but I don't want him owning you when it's time for the baby."

Sims got red in the face. He reached for the buggy whip, pulled it from the socket, and then he said, "I ought to lay this across your face, Gordon. Mike Dugan don't own me and don't you think he ever will." Then he slashed his horses across the rump and went careening down the road.

Tom returned to the house and sat down beside Bert's bed, knowing he had made a mistake with Sims. He said, "Bert, I've been thinking. Pete and me can handle the work here, and Arnie ought to be in school when it starts. Why don't I buy you out and you and Rose move to Eula? Take my lots and put up a livery stable. It'll give you a living, and it won't take the hard work you're going to have to do on the ranch."

Bert's gray face turned almost purple. He tried to raise himself on his elbows and fell back groaning; then he said, "Go to hell. I'm your partner and I aim to keep on being your partner."

Afterward Tom talked to Rose about it and she agreed it would have to be that way. When Tom came back from roundup, Bert was sitting in a rocking chair by a front window. Tom had been in and out of the house occasionally, but he had never mentioned the livery stable during that time.

Now Bert, knowing that roundup was over, and humiliated because he had not been able to get on a horse, said, "You're right, Tom. We'll move to town if you've got the money to buy me out. I'll take what I paid. It'll be enough to put a stable up and build a house that'll do for me'n Rose and Arnie. Hamilton was out the other day. He couldn't get the teacher he wanted, so he asked Rose to take the job. She said she would."

"I've got the money," Tom said, and understood how much it had cost Bert to say this.

chapter 24

As soon as Bert was able to walk, he moved to Eula with Rose and Arnie, and in spite of Arnie's howls of protest, Bert put him in school. Bert was able to work if he didn't keep at it too long, and if he was careful when he bent over. He hired a carpenter who had drifted into the valley early in the fall looking for work, and together they put up a small livery barn which could be added to later if business warranted it.

Bert still had the horses he had brought from the Lazy K. He traded a few to Tom for hay and hired Pete to haul the hay. The rest of the horses he took to town. He picked up a few old saddles and a rig from the livery stable in Starbuck, and then announced to Rose he was in business.

Arnie hated school, even with Rose teaching. He fought every boy in school the first week, pulled the girls' pigtails and got his face thoroughly scratched, and received three thrashings from Bert. As soon as school was out at four, he made a beeline for the stable where he cleaned out the stalls and exercised the horses. If it wasn't for that, he told Bert defiantly after his third whipping, he'd run away and he didn't give a damn if the coyotes ate him.

Bert started work on a house as soon as the stable was finished, having taken rooms in the hotel until he could move into the house. Rose divided the furniture they had brought from the Lazy K with Cynthia, skilfully maneuvering so that Cynthia kept most of her mother's treasured pieces and Rose took some of the furniture Harley Bangs had left on the Rafter T. If Bert realized what had happened, he never indicated it by word or gesture, and Rose, relieved when she saw that her trickery wasn't going to lead to trouble, told Tom she thought Bert was glad he didn't have to look at things that reminded him of his first wife.

Eddie Vance kept up a steady barrage of words in each issue of the *Herald* favoring Eula as a county seat over Starbuck. He mailed the paper free of charge to every rancher, dry-land farmer, and logger in the north half of the valley, telling them that after November first they could pay him the regular subscription price of two dollars a year in advance.

Vance expected to get a beating from some of Dugan's buckaroos, or shot, and he told Andrew Hamilton flatly that it was up to Hamilton and his partisans to keep him alive. This led to a secret organization called the 77 which met every Saturday night in Hamilton's bar and was a source of considerable revenue to Hamilton.

In addition, the 77 gave Vance the protection he wanted. An armed guard, carrying a pistol and a double-barreled shotgun loaded with buckshot, patrolled his print shop every night. Tom, not wanting to leave Cynthia, sent Pete to take his turn, a chore Pete was glad to do, for he was restless now that the pressure of work had eased up and he was happy for an excuse to spend a night in town.

On the morning of election day, the members of the 77 made it their job to get the vote out. They organized carefully and fanned out over the north half of the county, bringing in some dry-land farmers from the most distant corners of the county. Luck was on Eula's side, for a grass fire broke out east of the Two Medicine Peaks range that kept Sam Bell and his Arrow crew at home fighting desperately to save their buildings.

Tom, Andrew Hamilton, and Eddie Vance stayed at the polling place all day, keeping a record of those who voted. In the middle of the morning Dugan arrived with the Bar D crew. They voted, and then retired to the Red Bull Saloon. All of them except Todd Moody, Lew Roman, and a buckaroo named Turk Loman, returned to the Bar D. Apparently Dugan had delegated these three to watch the polls, but Roman spent more time than he should in the Red Bull. By evening he couldn't tell a Starbuck man from a Eula man.

Within fifteen minutes of closing time, Tom figured Eula had lost, but Alex Grimes and his son Terry arrived with a wagon-load of loggers from a camp near the head of Duck River. They hadn't wanted to come, having no real stake in the election, but a look at the muzzles of the Grimes' guns convinced them they should do their civic duty. Having come, they voted as they should, then moved to the Red Bull to celebrate. Before morning they had the saloon in shambles, Broncho Quinn having voted early and left town.

Eula won by three votes, the first defeat of the kind that Dugan and the Bar D had suffered. Tom expected trouble, but nothing happened. Todd Moody and Turk Loman dipped Lew Roman's head into the horse trough a few times, loaded him on his horse, and the three of them left town.

The rest of the night was quiet except for the loggers celebrating in the Red Bull. Riding back to Eula with

Tom and Eddie Vance, Hamilton opined that if any of the loggers swung an ax the next day, he'd cut his own leg off.

This was a defeat Dugan could not ignore, but the trouble Tom expected didn't come. Then he found out why. Dugan took it to court, claiming that at least eight of the Eula votes didn't count because the voters had not been residents of the county long enough to be eligible. Starbuck would win if those eight votes were thrown out. There the matter rested through the winter and spring, with Starbuck continuing as the county seat.

"Same old story," Hamilton said furiously. "He's got money to fight it through the courts till he gets another election. Next time there won't be a grass fire and Sam Bell and his boys will vote."

The 77 disbanded after the election, then reorganized secretly and carefully. From what Tom heard, Grimes and Hamilton were the leaders, and they wanted only men they could trust. This time Bert refused to have anything to do with it.

"They're crazy," he told Tom. "I pick up gossip now and then in the stable. Might not be anything to it, but the talk is that they're going after the Bar D some night. Cut fences. Burn haystacks. Even shoot Bar D stock."

Pete still belonged. Once in the middle of the winter Tom, sour-tempered because Pete rode off every Saturday night to the meetings regardless of weather or anything else, told him he'd do well to get out while he could.

"You've got a hell of a lot of right to tell me where to go on Saturday nights," Pete flung at him.

It was the nearest to a serious quarrel they'd had, and it worried Tom. He said mildly, "The only way to fight Dugan is to use his own methods. He's too big and important to operate the way he used to, beating up men like Corrigan, for instance. He'll use the law and the courts, and the only chance we've got is to vote Broncho Quinn out of office next fall."

"By that time you'll be broke if you don't sell some steers," Pete said.

Tom couldn't argue that point, for it was true. His cash reserve had melted alarmingly. "I'll figure out something," he said.

"I'd like to know what," Pete challenged. "If you had any sense, you'd come to our meetings. They'd listen to you. I'm the one who wants action, but they just sit and drink Hamilton's whisky and talk. A bunch of spit-'n-talk boys. That's all they are."

"I've never been invited."

"Hamilton told me to ask you; but you made your feelings mighty damned clear. So I never did."

"My feelings haven't changed," Tom said. "And you're lucky you're hooked up with a bunch of spit-'n-talk boys. The first raid you make, you'll be in jail."

Nothing happened until April, and when it did, the result was exactly what Tom had said it would be. Dugan's fence was cut in a dozen places and two Wineglass haystacks were burned. Apparently lots had been drawn as to who would do the raiding. At least Tom guessed it was that way, and Pete and Andrew Hamilton had lost, for both made an appearance in the Red Bull in Starbuck where they were seen by a dozen people. Pete even managed a fight with a Bar D hand.

Now Dugan was on solid ground. Broncho Quinn deputized Todd Moody and Turk Loman, quizzed around until he found out who couldn't account for himself the night of the trouble, and then arrested Terry Grimes and one of Harry Winch's hands named Raines. He had no evidence against them, but he threw them into jail and said they'd stay there until the grand jury met. They did, too, in spite of anything Alex Grimes could do.

Tom was irritated by the whole business because it weakened the position of the Eula group. He told Hamilton, "We'll wind up with a special investigator for the governor on our hands, and then where'll we be with Dugan's fence cut and his stacks burned?"

"Out there in Salem they don't know anybody but Mike Dugan lives in Indian Valley," Hamilton grumbled. "Time they found out different."

"You didn't answer my question," Tom said.

Hamilton didn't try. He turned and walked off.

Tom had too much on his mind to worry about young Grimes and Raines. There had been little snow during the winter and less rain in the spring, and by the time roundup was finished, Moon Creek was lower than it had been in years. Harry Winch said it was lower than he'd ever seen it, and he'd been living on the Cross 9 since right after the Piute trouble.

Tom's cattle came through the winter in excellent shape, and he had a good calf crop. The calves were branded, the stock on summer range, but it looked as if Tom wouldn't put up more than half the hay he had the summer before. He had some carryover from the previous year, but it would be tight if the next winter was a bad one.

In spite of himself he worried about Cynthia. Because he insisted, she had gone to Starbuck a few times to see Doc Sims, and he said she was in fine shape. Tom tried to get her to stay in Starbuck where she would be close to the doctor when her time came, but she refused. Then he wanted her to go to Eula to stay with Bert and Rose, but she refused even to do that.

"I've got housework to do and I'm going to do it." She sat down beside the kitchen table and fanned herself. "I'm better off to have work to do than just sit." She glanced at her swollen abdomen and shook her head. "I look a fright. I don't blame you for not wanting to have me around."

"It's not that," he said, irritated by her lack of understanding. "Pete and me are gone all day. Sometimes we aren't even here for dinner. If your time came, there wouldn't be anyone to go after the doc."

"Then I'd have the baby by myself," she said. "Cows do it all the time."

"Damn it, you're not a cow." He stopped, reminding himself that he'd heard pregnant women were difficult. But this was more than pregnancy, he thought. They had grown further apart through the winter, Cynthia preoccupied with her work and baby clothes, seldom asking about the ranch or even what Tom was doing. He searched his mind many times, trying to find where he had failed, or was at fault, but he never succeeded.

He hadn't been drunk since they were married, he didn't waste his money gambling, and he spent very little time in town. He saw to it that she was never out of wood, he carried water for her from the creek, and if she expressed a desire for something foolish the way pregnant women were notorious for doing, he tried to get it for her.

Now he thought with a sudden rush of bitterness that she should give him credit for these things, that she should realize she was lucky to have a steady husband and not someone like Harry Winch who regularly spent his Sunday nights with a whore who had recently moved to Starbuck.

But he couldn't bring himself to remind her of any of these things, so he said, "I'm worried about you. That's all."

"Well, don't be," she said tartly.

He rode to Eula that afternoon, thinking about his last months on the Bar D when he had been deeply in love with Bonnie and had thought so much about marriage, wanting it more than anything else; but it had been denied him. Now Bonnie was gone, he would probably never see her again, and he was married to

Cynthia, a marriage which was lacking in many ways when he set it in his mind against what he thought marriage should be.

He asked Rose to come out and stay with Cynthia until the baby came, and Rose said she would be glad to. He considered talking to Rose, trying to find out from her if the trouble was with him or Cynthia, and what he could do, but he couldn't bring himself to open the subject, admitting to himself that maybe he was afraid of the truth.

When he took Rose into the house and put her valise down, Cynthia screamed at him that she didn't need Rose or anyone. He walked out, his mood sour as he wondered if the next fifty years would be any worse. He thought of Bert's first wife, who apparently had not been happy with him, and he asked himself if Cynthia would ever turn to another man in a moment of passion, seeking a satisfaction he had never been able to give her.

Cynthia's pains started Saturday night just after Pete had left for one of his meetings. Rose said, "You'll have to go after the doctor. Tell him to hurry."

"What if he doesn't get here in time."

"I'll do the best I can," Rose said, "but right now you'd better hurry."

He threw his saddle on his sorrel that was fresh, not having been ridden for three days. The horse felt good and pitched a couple of times before Tom got him lined out, then he almost killed the animal riding to Starbuck. Sims was home and getting ready for bed.

202

"I'll be with you as soon as I dress," Sims said. "Go to the livery stable and harness up my horse."

Tom obeyed, but Sims didn't come. Tom paced back and forth in the runway, his pulse pounding, anxiety gnawing at him. When, after what seemed an eternity, Sims did come, Todd Moody and Turk Loman were with him.

"Might as well go home Tommy," Todd said, his tone as affable as ever. "Doc's going with us to Wineglass. Pablo got throwed by his horse and tromped some."

A splash of red washed across Tom's eyes as a crazy notion entered his mind that this was part of Dugan's scheming, that Dugan was determined to make him lose his wife and baby.

"I'll get to your place as soon as I can," Sims said with tightly drawn lips. "Todd's making me go with him."

"The hell he is," Tom shouted. "I got here first. You promised you'd—"

"I'm right sorry," Todd said, and from his tone it was plain he wasn't sorry at all. "It ain't our fault you knocked your wife up. Next time be more careful. All right, doc, let's travel.'

Tom lunged at Todd, the red waves beating against his eyes. He got a fist through to Todd's jaw, a solid blow that sent him reeling into the street through the archway, but he had forgotten Turk Loman. Loman's descending gun barrel caught Tom on the side of the head and knocked him cold. He fell face down into the barn litter.

Loman would have hit him again if Sims hadn't yelled, "You trying to kill him? You may have already."

"I'd as soon see him dead as not," Todd said, rubbing his jaw, "but not this way. Mike wouldn't like it. Roll him out of the way, Turk, and let's travel."

It was still dark when Tom came to. He got up and fell down again, and it was some time before the waves of nausea passed and he could stay on his feet. Gradually the memory of everything that had happened came back to him. Cynthia must have had the baby by now, but the doctor wouldn't have been with her.

He found the night man asleep in a back stall and shook him awake. "What happened?' Tom asked.

"I dunno." The hostler yawned. "Doc Sims left in his buggy with Moody and Loman. You was out cold, so I left you there."

Tom found his horse and rode back toward the Rafter T, his head pounding, but he didn't think of his pain. He kept thinking of Cynthia and the baby, and of the absence of the doctor, and of his certainty that Rose had never helped deliver a baby before.

It was dawn when he got back to the Rafter T and swung out of the saddle, reeling a little when he tried to walk. Pete came to him, saying, "I'll take care of your horse."

"Cynthia? The baby?"

Pete didn't say anything. Tom couldn't see his face clearly in the thin light, and when Pete didn't answer,

Tom grabbed his arm and shook him. "What happened?"

"The baby's dead," Pete said slowly, and then Tom realized he had been crying.

Tom went to the barn and sat down, his head between his knees. He was numb, too numb to think or feel, and it wasn't until Pete came to him that he thought about Cynthia. "Rose says sis is all right, but you're not to see her yet. God, Tom, it's been hard on her."

Tom still couldn't cry or curse or do anything except sit there as if he were paralyzed. The sun came up and Rose called breakfast, but he couldn't move. Presently he saw the doctor's rig come up the road, Sims plying his whip at every jump. He pulled to a stop, and yelled at Tom to look after his horse. Slowly Tom obeyed, moving mechanically, and later when Sims left the house, he said, "You can see her now, Gordon. Be easy with her, boy, be easy."

"She's all right?"

"She's all right. Nothing for me to do except clean her up. I don't know if I could have saved the baby or not."

Pete was coming out of the house. Tom swallowed, then he caught Sims by the shoulders. "Goddamn it, man, why didn't you come here first?"

"Why? You ought to know. Loman had a gun in my back. They came to the house right after you did." Sims pointed to the bruises on the side of his face. "They roughed me up some."

Tom dropped his hands. He should have known. He said, "What are you going to do about it?"

"I'm moving to Eula. Today. Now go see her."

Tom walked across the hard bare yard, stumbling a little, his toes dragging. A lamp still burned in the front room. He went on into their bedroom. The lamp on the bureau beside the Waterbury clock was still lighted, too. He pulled a chair up to the bed, and then he looked at her for the first time, not aware that Rose was standing a few feet from him.

Cynthia seemed very small, lying in the big bed with her black hair covering most of the pillow. He had never seen her face as pale as it was now, or as tired looking.

Then it hit him, a wave of tenderness for her that he had never felt before, and the tears came, and he cried as he had not cried for many years, his head tipped forward. Rose came to him and put a hand on his shoulder.

"I tried to get the doctor," he said. "I tried."

"We know," Rose said. "He told us."

"We'll have another baby," Cynthia whispered. "You'll see."

"I love you," he said.

Cynthia's hand came out and touched him on the cheek. She whispered, "Tom, that's the first time you ever said you loved me."

He knew, then, where the fault had been.

chapter 25

CYNTHIA'S RECOVERY WAS SLOW but without serious setbacks. Doc Sims came out every day for a while, then every other day. He had moved to Eula as he had promised. Every time Tom saw the ugly bruises on the doctor's face, he told himself he had been a fool to think Sims could have done anything than what he had.

Tom realized that he had been equally foolish to think that Todd Moody and Turk Loman had been waiting for the particular moment when Cynthia needed a doctor. It had been an accident that they had arrived at Sims's home a few minutes after he had. But it had not been an accident that they had used force to make Sims go with them, no accident that Todd Moody had made the decision that Pablo Garcia's life was more important than that of Cynthia and her baby.

Tom had this matter on his mind a great deal for the next three weeks as soon as he was able to think coherently. Even more important than the loss of his baby and the possible loss of Cynthia's life was this casual manner in which the Bar D played God.

Todd Moody had made the decision, but Mike Dugan would have made the same decision. It was the way he had trained his men to think. There was no equality in Starbuck County. Rather, there were the first-class citizens who had prior rights, the people who belonged to Bar D. Everybody else had second-class citizenship. Like Cynthia and the baby, they could take what was left.

So, in the end, Tom reached the only conclusion he could after what had happened. The time of waiting was done. He knew there was no sense in going back over what had happened, but still he was plagued by the thought that if he had not waited so long his son might be alive. He knew it was wrong thinking. The time had not come to make a move against Dugan. If he had, he would have played into Dugan's hands and ruined whatever chance there was of defeating him.

Small, annoying acts like the fence-cutting and hay-burning were no more effective than a fly buzzing around a horse's ear. Terry Grimes and Harry Winch's man Raines had been released from jail for lack of evidence, but on the other hand they hadn't accomplished anything either. Still, the sense that he had not done all that he should weighed upon his conscience.

Once having made the decision to force the issue with Dugan, he was goaded by impatience. As soon as Cynthia had her strength back, Tom told Pete on a Saturday night after supper that he wanted to go with him to the meeting of the 77. Apparently Pete had been expecting it, for he slapped Tom on the back as he said, "It's about time. Last meeting Andrew Hamilton told me to fetch you along, but I said I was damned if I'd ask you again."

"I want your pa to be at this meeting, too," Tom said.

Pete backed up a step, the good humor leaving his

face. "I dunno about that. He's kind o' like a fire-cracker that's been out in the wet."

"We'll dry him out," Tom said. "You saddle up. I'll tell Cynthia I'm going to town."

"There's something else," Pete said slowly. "Now that you've finally decided to move, I don't want you backing down for any reason. So maybe you'd better know. Bonnie's back."

Tom glanced sharply at Pete. "Why should that make any difference?"

"Break Dugan and you might break her, too. She's back because she's a widow and she's Dugan's daughter. She's also someone you cared about once."

Tom shook his head. "Not any more. Bonnie never really cared about anyone but herself. She learned it from Dugan. She picked his side a long time ago. Come to that, I've made my choice too. What happens to you and Bert and Cynthia is more important to me than anything Bonnie ever was."

Pete nodded. "I just wanted to be sure."

Tom had a sudden understanding of how much faith the younger man was putting in him. He grinned. "Don't worry, Pete. Your pa and me will be all right." He headed quickly for the house.

Rose was still there, although she would be leaving soon. Cynthia was able to do the housework as long as she didn't let herself get too tired. Both women were sitting on the porch as Tom came up.

Cynthia was talking to Rose, but when she heard him, she turned her head to smile at him, and again the feeling of tenderness for her rushed over him and made it impossible for him to speak for a moment.

He leaned down and kissed her, and asked, "How do you feel?"

"Fine," she answered, "except that I'm ashamed of myself for being so lazy. You and Rose baby me too much."

"Not much longer," Rose said. "I'll be going back to Eula the first of the week."

"I'm riding into town tonight with Pete," Tom said casually. "Don't wait up for me."

He saw quick alarm in Rose's face and he wanted to shake his head at her, but Cynthia was looking at him and he couldn't. Rose caught herself in time, and she said, "Tell Bert I'll see him in a day or two."

He nodded, still trying to be casual. He said, "I'll tell him," and swung around and walked back across the yard.

It was dusk when they reached Eula. Tom was impressed with the way the town had grown from the time he had first seen it nearly a year ago when it had consisted only of Hamilton's store, his house, and dozens of "For Sale" signs. A few of the signs were still up around the fringe of the buildings, but now Eula had as many people as Starbuck, and with the exception of a bank, as many businesses.

He turned into the livery stable, saying, "You tell Hamilton I'll be along in a minute. Bert's going to be with me."

"He won't like it," Pete said. "He figures he's the

210

big mogul and he has to pass on everybody."

"Tell him I'm going to pass on him," Tom said.

He dismounted, leaving his sorrel in the runway, and found Bert currying a horse in the third stall. He said, "Howdy, Bert. How's your back?"

A lantern hanging from a rafter threw a poor light over the interior of the stable so that Bert didn't know who had come in until he heard Tom's voice. Then he said, "Oh, hello, Tom. Pretty good if I'm careful. When's Rose coming home? How's Cynthia?"

"Two questions, so you'll get two answers. Rose said she'd see you in a day or two, and Cynthia is fine as long as she doesn't get too ambitious. Bert, it strikes me that a man with a bad back is better off without a wife for a while."

Tom thought he was being funny, but from the expression on Bert's face, he realized he had been the opposite. Bert went on brushing the back of the horse for a moment, then he said with some bitterness, "Doesn't make much difference about my back any more. I'm just not much man."

"You will be tonight. I want you to harness up your fastest team, hook up to the wagon, and drive to the store. We're joining the 77. We've got a job to do before morning."

Bert stepped into the runway, his brush in one hand, the curry comb in the other. He hesitated, having no liking for this business, then he said, "Time to kick the lid off, is it?"

"It's past time," Tom said. "Bring your Winchester."

"It'll take me ten minutes or so," Bert said. "Arnie's in the back watering the horses. I'll have to tell him to stay here till I get back."

"It'll be late."

"There's a cot in the office he can sleep on," Bert said, and plodded along the runway to the back door.

Tom mounted and turning into the street, rode to the store, wondering what Ben Lampe would say if he could see Bert Mayer now. Tom had known Bert for nearly eleven years, and in that time he had watched the steady deterioration of a man.

He found ten men lounging along the bar in Hamilton's store: Hamilton, Alex Grimes and his two oldest sons, Harry Winch and his buckaroo Duke Raines who had been jailed with Terry Grimes, Pete, and three small cowmen from the hills north of Moon Creek. It struck Tom that there were no townsmen except Hamilton, and none of the dry farmers east of Duck River.

Tom shook hands with all of them. They seemed genuinely glad to see him. Some said he was mighty slow coming around, and others remarked about him carrying his revolver, which he seldom did, and that made him wonder if Cynthia had seen it before he'd left home. She hadn't commented on it, so she probably hadn't noticed.

When the social amenities were disposed of, Tom said, "Andy, I'd like to talk to you and Alex for a minute."

Hamilton glanced at Grimes, hesitated, then nodded,

and crossed the big room to the dry-goods counter on the opposite side, Tom following. Grimes came in the rear, blowing and puffing as he did every time he moved the great mass of flesh that was his body.

"I've got two things on my mind," Tom said. "Number one. If we threw our steers into one herd this fall and didn't turn them over to Dugan, could we swing out into the desert and keep west of Bar D range and get them to Winnemucca?"

"No," Grimes said quickly. "It's too far, there's not enough water that time of year, and not enough grass. We'd have walking skeletons by the time we got 'em to Winnemucca."

"All right then. Could we go east of the Two Medicine Peaks range and take them through Sam Bell's range?"

"No," Grimes said. "Sam Bell wouldn't stand for it. He's closer to Dugan than Harry Winch is to that damned whore when he gets into bed with her."

"Then the only thing we can do," Tom said, "is to make Broncho Quinn open the county road through Bar D range."

"He won't do it," Hamilton said.

"He will once he knows we've got the votes," Tom said. "He's looking ahead to the election next fall. But that can wait. The second thing I've got in mind can't. Andy, have you heard anything from the Supreme Court on the county-seat business?"

"Just got word from our lawyer in Salem," Hamilton said. "I was waiting for you to get here so I could tell the boys, but I'll tell you now. We won by two votes."

"Then we can go ahead with moving the county seat here," Tom said. "I wish we had built a courthouse, but we didn't, so we'll have to use the hotel rooms for temporary offices. Maybe the rooms you've got overhead, Andy."

"That's what I was aiming—"

"Now there's one thing that's not going to set well with you two," Tom broke in. "Alex here has been running the show and he's done nothing to hit Dugan where it hurts. Andy, you've been talking and selling whisky every Saturday night, so you've shown a profit from the time the 77 was started."

"Well by God," Hamilton said, his face turning red. "If you ain't got the gall of a—"

"Sure I have," Tom agreed. "Now Pete tells me this is a spit-'n-talk bunch. Well, the time of spitting and talking is over. We've got to move and move tonight. I propose to give the orders. The first one is that Bert Mayer goes with us."

"Not by a damned sight he don't," Hamilton said hotly. "If you think you can walk in here and—"

"I don't only think it," Tom said. "I will. I've wondered about you, Andy. Most of us have good personal reasons for whittling Dugan down. You've never given us yours, but I'd say you came here to make a fistful of money. You figured you could do it by taking sides against Dugan, but if you were careful, you wouldn't make him mad enough to hit back. Well, you've been so careful you haven't done anything. It wouldn't surprise me if you'd heard about that court decision two weeks ago."

Hamilton was so furious he was incoherent, but Grimes laughed and slapped the counter with a fat hand. "It was three weeks, Tom, but he held it back. Kept saying it wasn't time to tell it." He jerked his head at Hamilton. "Come on, Andy. He's right. We're out and he's in." He started across the room to the others, saying, "Time's running out. Give us your orders, Tom."

Hamilton was talking to himself, but he followed. Grimes pounded the bar, nodding at Bert who had just come in. "Tom Gordon says it's time we're doing something besides spit and talk, and making Andy rich drinking his whisky. Tom's right, so from now on he's the general. What do we do, Tom?"

"We'll have no more hay-burning," Tom said. "That puts us on the wrong side of the law. Dugan's maneuvered himself into position to use the courts and the sheriff. He can wait us out. If he waits long enough, we're whipped, so I propose to fight him with his own weapons and keep the law on our side."

All the men including Hamilton nodded agreement except Harry Winch who began to back away. "I don't think I want—"

"You will, Harry," Tom said. "You'll stand with us right down the line or we'll make it so tough for you that you'll sell out to Alex for a song and get out of the country. Now wipe that tobacco juice off your chin and listen to me. Tonight we're moving the county records to Eula. It'll be midnight when we get there. If Dugan's boys are in town, we'll have a fight. We may anyhow if the Starbuck men decide to kick up some dust, but we'll be within our rights. The second thing we'll do is to start out Monday morning and we'll cut Dugan's north gate that blocks the county road. We'll go down that road past Wineglass and past the lakes and right past the Bar D buildings, and we'll cut every God-damned gate there is between here and Winnemucca, and I'll see that Broncho Quinn is with us while we're doing it."

They cheered him and laughed and pounded each other on the back, and Pete yelled, "I told you this would happen if we ever got old Tom here."

Only Harry Winch looked as if he wished he were someplace else. Even Hamilton was excited. Tom shot a glance at Bert and saw sharp interest in his face. It looked as though Bert Mayer would be all right.

"Just one thing before we start," Tom said. "No shooting until I give the word, and I won't give the word unless they force a fight on us. I don't think they will. I think we can pull this off without a shot being fired. Before we start, I want all of you to wrap the metal on your rigs so we won't have anything banging away to warn 'em. We can't keep the wagon from squealing, but I don't think a wagon will worry anybody if they don't hear a bunch of riders, too. Bert will back the wagon up to the front door of the courthouse. Andy, give us some rags. Better throw a bunch of boxes into the wagon bed. We'll pile the records into 'em and that way we won't take any chance on losing some of 'em. I'll get Broncho there to see it's done legally. I'm going ahead. The rest of you stay with the wagon. Go right to the courthouse."

"I've got some rags in the back room," Hamilton said. "Plenty of boxes, too."

Tom went out through the front, winking at Bert who winked back. There was none of the whipped-dog look about him now. He'd do, Tom thought, and so would all of them except Harry Winch. It had been a mistake to bring Winch into the organization in the first place, but that had been Grimes's or Hamilton's doing, not his.

When he reached Starbuck, he saw that the town was dark except for the Red Bull Saloon. He left his horse at the end of the block, and keeping in the shadows, reached the front of the saloon and looked through a window. There were six men inside besides the bartender. Four were Bar D hands. He didn't know the other two. But neither Moody nor Turk Loman was there, and they were the men he was worried about.

He slipped back along the street, thankful there was no moon tonight. He got Quinn out of bed and made him dress, his cocked gun on the big man's belly. Quinn cursed and threatened, and said Dugan would have their hides for this.

"Broncho," Tom said, "You're a politician, so there's one thing you know as well as I do. By fall Dugan won't be able to swing enough votes to elect you or anyone else. Pick your side now and do it quick."

Quinn didn't argue any more. He was waiting with Tom in front of the courthouse when Bert got there with the wagon. He unlocked the door and lighted a lamp. Then, his face red, he said, "Gentlemen, we're moving the county seat to Eula according to the will of the people as indicated in the election last fall, and as confirmed by the recent decision of the Supreme Court of the sovereign state of Oregon."

Tom wanted to laugh. He had never expected to hear a speech like that from Broncho Quinn. Tom, Pete, and Duke Raines deployed into a half circle, listening and moving around quietly, but if the Bar D men heard, they ignored it and kept on playing poker. About one o'clock they left town and the lights in the Red Bull went out. And if a townsman heard, he turned over and went on sleeping.

There was a constant procession moving in and out of the courthouse. Men talked, the fear of a fight gone now. Doors were slammed. The stairs squeaked. Men grunted under the weight of a safe they lifted into the wagon. By two they were done, Broncho Quinn having worked as hard as any man. The wagon rolled out of town, Quinn riding next to the tailgate to be sure that nothing slid out.

They stored the papers in the Eula schoolhouse to be transferred later when the county officials moved to Eula from Starbuck and space was allotted to each of them in the hotel and Hamilton's store. Before the group broke up at dawn, Tom said, "Be here at ten Monday morning and we'll cut Dugan's gates. Broncho, you'll furnish the wire clippers, won't you?"

Quinn hesitated, then grinned feebly. "Sure, and I'll do the squeezing, if that'll make it legal, but I'll tell you boys something. Mike Dugan may overlook the chore we done tonight, but he won't overlook cutting his gates."

On the way home, Pete yawned, and said happily, "Well, we opened the ball. It's Dugan's turn now."

"He'll do something, too," Tom said. "Before Monday morning if my hunch is right."

"What'll he do?"

"I don't know. I wish I did."

But he was satisfied with what had been accomplished and didn't worry about what Dugan would do. He fell across the bed as soon as he got home and dropped off to sleep at once, feeling at peace with himself for the first time in months. He was sleeping so soundly that he was not aware when Cynthia slipped into the room and lay down beside him, her arm flung lightly over his shoulders.

chapter 26

CYNTHIA WOKE TOM LATE on Sunday morning. He stared at her, asking grumpily why she couldn't let him sleep. He had never felt so tired in his life.

"I'm sorry," she said. "I had to wake you. Pete took Rose into Eula early and now he's back with news."

When Tom reached the yard, Pete didn't waste any time. He said, "Dugan's making his move. He's coming to Eula to hang Hamilton and Grimes and you."

"Is he in Eula now?"

"Not when I left. Terry Grimes went to Starbuck this morning to wind up a horse trade with the livery stable that he's been working on for a week or more. He was in the Red Bull when Dugan showed up with some of his crew. That's what they were saying they were going to do, so Terry slid out through the back door and lit a shuck for Eula. Pa sent me to fetch you and I'm going on into the hills to get some more help. Terry went home to get the rest of the Grimes bunch, and they'll get Harry Winch and Raines, too. But hell, we'll be too late."

Cynthia tugged at Tom's arm. "I'm going to town with you. I won't be left behind to worry about you."

"Better take her," Pete said. "Eddie Vance and pa were talking. They think Dugan is running a sandy on us. He'll wait till we all get to town, then they'll come up the creek and burn us out. That'd break our backs, all right, and nobody could prove they done it."

"I'll be safer in town with you than here," Cynthia said, and tugged at his arm again.

Tom started toward the cart as Pete said, "You'd better travel. They need you in town. That bunch is about as tough as a herd of rabbits."

Tom stopped. "Did Terry tell you how many men Dugan had?"

"Yeah, and that's something else I don't savvy," Pete said. "He could have fetched twenty men, but there was only six of 'em: Turk Loman, Todd, Lew, and a couple Terry didn't know. And Dugan."

Tom went on toward the cart then, gave Cynthia a hand up, and then sat beside her. They started down the slope, leaving the road along the creek and quartering across the grass directly toward Eula. This way was rougher than the road, but it saved more than a mile.

He couldn't expect any speed out of the mare. Pete had driven her too hard. Maybe it would have been better if Tom had hooked up another animal, but the mare was the only one they ever used on the cart. Besides, the work horses were in the pasture and it would have taken time to bring them in.

Something kept nudging Tom's mind that he couldn't quite pin down. To his way of thinking, it didn't make sense for Dugan to come to Starbuck with a handful of men and state his intention when a known Eula man was in the saloon. Obviously they wanted young Grimes to take word to Eula or they wouldn't have let him slip out through the back door.

The whole operation made Dugan look stupid or careless, but whatever failings the man had, neither stupidity nor carelessness was one of them. Pete's notion might be right, that Dugan wanted his principal enemies concentrated in Eula so he could burn their ranches. After a moment's thought, Tom discarded that theory.

Dugan operated with a set pattern, ignoring his opposition as long as he could, counting on various oblique pressures to win his point. When he reached the place where he had to make a move, as he undoubtedly had now, he struck directly at the heart of his enemies. Eula was that heart.

Whether it was the moving of the county records to Eula or the threat of cutting the gates Monday morning that had impelled Dugan to act was a question. In any case, Eula was the objective, but why had he purposely given his enemies a warning?

Tom backtracked in his mind, certain that Dugan's purpose was the destruction of Eula, but along with that he would certainly hope to kill the leaders of his opposition. But he couldn't afford to murder them outright. He was bound to work it so that it would appear he was within the law. To the courts, and the governor if he took a hand, the law in Starbuck County was Broncho Quinn, and Broncho Quinn was in Eula.

These were the facts, laid out in Tom's mind as clearly as he could lay them. He was certain that the answer was right here at his fingertips, but he was more than halfway to Eula when it came to him. When it did, it seemed perfectly clear, and he wondered why he hadn't thought of it sooner.

Dugan had made his threat in Starbuck, but it had been only a threat. If the case ever came to court, he could deny he had made a threat. He could dismiss it as being scare talk on the part of Terry Grimes, and nobody could prove otherwise. The bartender in the

Red Bull was as much a Dugan man as the Bar D crew.

But the threat had been made, so when Dugan and his buckaroos rode into Eula, all it would take was for some trigger-happy Eula man to fire a shot and the fight would be started, with the Bar D men shooting back in self-defense. Before it was over, Eula would be destroyed, and probably Grimes, Hamilton, and Tom Gordon would be dead.

The solution, then, was to see to it that no one on the Eula side fired the first shot. Here was the answer to why Dugan had not brought more men. If he rode in with his whole outfit, the odds would be so great that the fight wouldn't start. Eula would simply be evacuated and Dugan would accomplish only half his objective. As it was, Dugan was confident that his half-dozen men could handle the entire north half of Starbuck County if it came to that, and Tom wasn't sure he was wrong.

They were in Eula then, and he saw the line of horses tied in front of Hamilton's store. It was the only saloon in town, so it was the natural place for the Bar D men to go. They had been drinking in Starbuck and if they started drinking now, it might get out of hand before Dugan realized it; particularly with Lew Roman, who might be drunk enough to do something wild and crazy in the hope of getting back into Dugan's favor.

Bert stood in the archway of his stable. When he saw Tom, he motioned to him and Tom drove through the archway. Rose was there, and Arnie. Tom stepped down and gave Cynthia a hand. She went at once to Rose, who said, "I'm glad Tom brought you. I don't know what's going to happen, but at least you'll be here and you'll know."

Bert told Arnie to take care of the mare. Then he said, "Six of them yonder in Hamilton's store. They rode in about half an hour ago, but they haven't done anything. What do you suppose they're up to?"

"They're waiting for us to open the ball," Tom said. "Where's Broncho?"

"He's with them, the son of a bitch. We'll be wiped out if Pete and young Grimes don't bring help."

"We'll be wiped out anyway if it starts," Tom said. "We haven't got enough men we can count on. Where's Hamilton and Eddie Vance and Doc Sims and the rest?"

"Yonder." Bert motioned toward the hotel. "Hamilton lit out of the store the minute they came in and they let him go." Bert shook his head, frowning. "You're sure right about not having many men to count on. There's not a fighting man in that bunch."

This sounded strange, coming from Bert. Tom glanced at his face, as gray as ever, but tight-lipped and grim, too. He'd do, once the shooting started. His rifle was leaning against the wall beside the archway, and that reminded Tom that he'd left his at home. He swore softly as Arnie came toward them, skipping along as he did when he was excited.

224

"We'll give 'em hell, won't we, Tom?" Arnie asked.

"Sure we will," Tom said, "only you stay with Rose and Cynthia. This looks like man business."

Arnie was insulted, but before he could say anything, Bonnie stepped out of the small room in the corner of the stable that was Bert's office. She said, "Hello, Tommy."

He whirled, shocked by her presence. In the brief instant his gaze met hers, he remembered a girl of sixteen he'd left five years before. But this woman standing before him was another person. She had no business here, and he was instantly angry because she complicated a situation whose lines he had thought were clearly drawn.

"What are you doing here?" he demanded abruptly.

She looked faintly surprised. "Why, I came to see you, Tommy," she said. "And Rose, of course."

"You're either foolish or pig-headed," he said. "Or maybe you're still trying to prove something. I don't know and I don't particularly care. Either way, you don't belong here and you know it. Get back over to the store where you belong."

Rose and Cynthia were standing behind her, both embarrassed and uncertain. Bert cleared his throat. "Now wait a minute, Tom. . . ."

"Not very polite, is he, Bert?" Bonnie said, amused.

This was a different Bonnie than the girl he had known, Tom thought. The girl Bonnie would have wept or exploded, but this woman stood poised and completely sure of herself.

225

"As a matter of fact, Tommy," Bonnie went on, "you're not even nearly right. You're the ones who don't belong here. You and Bert, of all people, should know you can't stand up to Mike Dugan. Why don't you give up and get out?"

Now her claws were beginning to show. Tom asked, "Did Dugan send you over here with that message?"

"No. That was my idea. I don't want any of you to get killed. Dad's idea is different. He doesn't intend for any of you to get away. Except Arnie. He wants Arnie. He figures you aren't so stubborn that you'd let his son get shot just to prove a point." She turned to the boy. "You know, Arnie, we're brother and sister. I don't suppose anyone ever told you that."

"You're lying," Arnie yelled. "Old Dugan ain't my pa. A lot of kids told me that after we moved here, and I beat hell out of 'em for saying it."

Tom started toward Bonnie, intent on silencing her if he had to knock her down, but before he reached her, she said, "Why do you think dad went to the Lazy K that time to get you if he wasn't your father, Arnie? He's always wanted a son, but he couldn't admit you were, so that was the only way he could—"

Rose was closer to Bonnie than Tom. She reached Bonnie first, her right hand swinging up and slapping the younger woman across the mouth. Tom's attention was fixed on Bonnie, and Bert's, too, so that neither noticed Arnie grab Bert's rifle from where it leaned against the wall and run into the street.

"Come back," Cynthia screamed. "Arnie, come back."

She was the only one who was aware of what was happening, but she had been too far from the door to stop the boy. Now he was running into the dusty street, yelling, "Dugan, come out of there, you son of a bitch. Come out and fight. I'm gonna kill you."

Tom started after the boy, but he was too late. Arnie was almost to the store when someone from inside fired. Arnie cried out in pain and stumbled and fell headlong into the dust.

Two more shots hammered out from inside the store, and Tom, running toward the wounded boy, wondered why he hadn't been hit, why bullets weren't kicking up dust in the street all around him.

chapter 27

BY THE TIME TOM REACHED ARNIE, the boy was on his hands and knees and crawling across the street, leaving a path of blood in the dust. He was whimpering in pain as Tom picked him up and started toward the hotel on the run, shouting at Bert who was coming toward him, "See if doc's inside. If he isn't, get him."

"He's there," Bert shouted back. "I saw him go in a while ago."

The front door of the hotel opened and Doc Sims motioned for Tom to come on. Tom's attention was fixed so sharply on the boy in his arms that he was almost to the hotel before he realized that Cynthia, Rose, and Bonnie were running toward him from the

227

livery stable, holding their long skirts above their knees, and that the Bar D bunch had rushed out of the store, Dugan in the lead.

As he went through the door, Dugan, who had caught up with him, demanded, "Is he hit bad, Gordon?"

Tom didn't answer. Sims was standing beside a leather couch in the lobby and motioning for Tom to lay the boy down. The lobby was jammed with townsmen, and Hamilton was shouting and shoving as he tried to clear a passage for Tom. Dugan, staying at Tom's elbow, said, "God, I didn't want this to happen."

Behind him Todd Moody said, "Lew was pretty drunk, Mike. He didn't know what he was doing."

And Turk Loman, at Todd's elbow, said, "He'll never find out, neither. Mike's last bullet got him right above his left eye."

Tom put the boy down on the couch. Sims, angry, said, "Get back, damn it, get back."

The crowd retreated, all but Rose, who kicked and elbowed her way through the men until she reached the couch. Hamilton kept pushing and saying there wouldn't be any more trouble, and finally got most of the townsmen outside where they milled around uncertainly. But Dugan wouldn't back up. The purple splotches on his face had turned black, and the pulse in his temples was throbbing with great trip-hammer beats.

Dugan stood motionless, staring at Arnie who was

groaning and writhing on the couch. Sims motioned for Bert to come to him. "Hold his shoulders down if you can. I've got to get the bleeding stopped."

Arnie had been hit in the leg. Sims had slit his pants from the waist all the way down and was trying to get a tourniquet into place. Then Dugan, unable to stand it any longer, called out, "Is it bad, doc?"

"Bad enough," Sims said without looking around, "but he'll be all right if I can keep him from bleeding to death."

It seemed crazy and illogical to Tom for Dugan to be as concerned as he was. He had never before seen the man bothered about anyone or anything except himself or Bonnie or the Bar D, and now Tom turned on him, filled with outrage.

"You think it was Lew Roman who did this?" Tom demanded. "It wasn't. It was you. You wanted a son, but when you had one, you left him for Bert to raise because you weren't honest enough to claim him. You knew he was in town today and your sister was here, too, but you brought your bunch in anyway figuring on wiping us out. Don't blame a drunk you kept on your payroll that you should have fired a long time ago. Put the blame where it belongs. You killed Arnie if he dies, and all the money you've got won't help you to forget it."

Silence then except for Arnie's groaning on the couch, and Dugan's breathing as he stared at Tom. He was a stricken man, all the raw strength and brutal power stripped from him. It came to Tom now, the memory of what Bert Mayer had said many times, that Dugan's sins would catch up with him, that in time a man must reap what he sows.

The time had come, and Tom had some hint of the pride Dugan had taken in Arnie, perhaps even affection and the hope that someday the boy would come to him. But there was no sympathy in Tom for this man who by one means or another had contrived to ruin dozens of people's lives. Tom thought of Ben Lampe and Dora Lind, of Arnie's mother and Bert, of Corrigan, of Rose and Bonnie . . . yes, even Bonnie.

Dugan was having trouble breathing. He raised a hand to his throat as if trying to help his laboring lungs, then he turned ponderously and started toward the door.

Tom opened his mouth to say more. There was more to be said, much more that no one had ever had the courage to say to Mike Dugan, but the words didn't leave Tom's throat. Dugan took two steps and collapsed, falling as if all control had gone from his legs. The sound was that of a great weight hitting the floor, and then blank silence until a strange, strangled *Ah* went up from the people in the room as if they had seen something that could not have happened.

Sims glanced around and turned back to Arnie. For some reason which Tom never understood, he was the first to go to Dugan, and kneeling beside him, felt of his pulse. Todd Moody and Turk Loman and the others, even Bonnie, stood motionless, staring at Dugan. Tom couldn't find the pulse, but he was inexperienced at it, and he wasn't sure he was feeling in the right place on Dugan's wrist.

"I think he's dead," Tom said.

"Turn him over," Sims said, and a moment later finished with Arnie. "You be quiet, son. You'll be all right if you don't start the bleeding again. That's just what you'll do if you keep faunching around."

As Sims walked to Dugan and knelt beside him, he said, "It wouldn't be surprising if he was dead. He never wanted anyone to know he came to me, thinking it was a sign of weakness, and Mike Dugan never wanted people to think he was weak about anything. He's had a bad heart for almost six years, and I told him it would kill him if he didn't quit shoving folks around and getting excited himself."

Sims picked up Dugan's wrist, felt for the pulse and nodded. "He's not dead," he said as if he regretted it. He examined Dugan's eyes carefully, then rose. "He's had a stroke. Pick him up and put him in bed."

Tom took Dugan's legs and Todd Moody his shoulders. They carried him to a bedroom in the rear of the hotel and laid him down. Bonnie followed with Turk Loman. No one else came until Sims joined them a moment later.

Sims made no effort to examine Dugan again. He looked down at him, chewing on his lower lip, then turned to Bonnie. "There's nothing I can do. He may live a long time, but he'll take a lot of attention because he'll be helpless. He may be able to talk someday. Just a little, kind of thick-lipped. Possibly he may even sit up and get around in a wheel chair, but outside of a miracle, he'll never ride a horse again."

"What'll happen to the Bar D?" Todd Moody asked, his voice shaking a little.

"I don't give a good, thin damn," Sims said harshly, "but I hope it goes broke."

"It won't," Bonnie said. "Can he understand what I'm saying? Is he conscious?"

"I think so," Sims said, "but he doesn't have any way of communicating with you."

"I just want him to know that Bar D won't break up," she said. "He's always accused me of not caring anything about the ranch, but he was wrong. It's a good thing I'm here because I'll see there's a good man running it. That's you, Tom. You know the layout. You know cattle. You know men and you can give orders. You and Cynthia can move into the house. I don't plan to spend much time there. As far as your salary goes, you can name it, but whatever it is, I'll guarantee it'll be more than you'll ever make off that greasy-sack spread you've got up there on Moon Creek."

"The hell," Todd blurted. "I'm the man to run Bar D."

"You?" Bonnie said witheringly. "I wouldn't trust you with a band of sheep if I ever got low enough to own a band of sheep. Or you, either, Loman. Neither one of you can get along with Bar D's neighbors, and Tom can."

She didn't mean it, Tom thought. She knew that

Mike Dugan would rather have any man alive run Bar D than him. Even Bert Mayer. She was saying this only to hurt Dugan who was helpless and unable to strike back for the first time in his life.

Staring at the man, it seemed to Tom his eyes were trying to protest, to say what he wanted to say with his lips, that his lips were actually moving. But if they were, no sound came from his throat.

Tom turned and walked back to the lobby. Rose and Cynthia were sitting beside the couch. Bert was gone. Tom said, "Nothing we can do, so guess we might as well mosey. Don't get any more big ideas, Arnie. You had one too many."

Arnie tried to grin. "I guess so, but I got so damned tired of hearing that Dugan was my pa I couldn't stand it. He ain't, and I'm never gonna have anything to do with him."

"You're ours, Arnie," Rose said softly. "Bert's and mine."

"Sure," Arnie said. "I know who my pa is, all right, and I know my real ma's dead, but you took her place, Rose. As good as anybody."

Cynthia leaned down and kissed him. "I'll be back in a day or two to see how you are," she said.

"When that bunged-up leg heals," Tom said, "you come out and stay with us. We'll go fishing."

He winked at the boy and turned away, taking Cynthia's arm. Rose said, "Bert's out trying to find something to move Arnie on."

"I'll see him in a day or so," Tom said.

Bonnie was waiting at the door. She hadn't given up, Tom saw, so he said, "It wouldn't work, Bonnie. Let's forget it."

"No," she said as if she thought she could brush away all opposition by her tone. "It would work. No strings attached, Tom." She looked at Cynthia. "Did he tell you?"

"No," Cynthia said.

"I've offered him a job managing Bar D. I said he could name his salary. He owes it to himself and to you. To everybody in the county. He could see to it that there's no more pushing and gouging and trying to make Bar D bigger. It's big enough."

For a moment Tom was tempted. She had said the one thing that appealed to him. The Bar D would not be a threat if he managed it. He looked at Bonnie, remembering how she had been as a child. Her father would bring her a doll from Winnemucca and for a time she would love it and play with it, and then she was done. She'd throw it away and never glance at it again.

He realized then that she had not been trying to be cruel to her father as much as she was trying to bend Tom to her will. Once she had him on the Bar D, she would try to come between him and Cynthia, perhaps get him back up on the shoulder of North Medicine Peak where they had been that afternoon. Or take advantage of some occasions when Cynthia was in town with Rose and her father. If Bonnie ever succeeded in having him again, she would be done with him and she'd throw him away just as she used to throw her dolls away. She was as predatory as her father; to her the fun was in the pursuing.

He shook his head, knowing that no good would come of it. "Maybe all I've got is a greasy-sack spread," he said, "but it's mine." He looked past her at Todd. "Monday morning we're opening every gate on the county road. If there's going to be trouble, I want. . . ."

"No trouble," Broncho Quinn said from the doorway. "I've told him."

Todd stared at Tom, sullenly silent. He was worried, Tom thought, and maybe scared, for Mike Dugan had been the source of strength to everyone on the Bar D. Now, like a spring in time of drought, the source of strength had dried up.

If Bonnie meant what she said, Todd would not be a part of Bar D's future. That was something he could not stand, and he would blame Tom for it. He had been the right arm of Mike Dugan too long. Men who were loyal to Bar D were never thrown overboard, and Todd had been loyal even by Dugan's exacting definition of the word.

Tom met Todd's gaze, trying to read the expression on the man's face, and failing. He could see nothing beyond the sullenness that stemmed from a sense of injury and hurt pride, and Tom wondered if Bonnie could make her decision stick, if Todd would defy her and remain on the Bar D. But that was her worry, not his. He nodded at Quinn, and taking Cynthia's arm again, moved through the door, Quinn stepping out of the way.

"Cynthia!" Bonnie's voice turned them. "Make him take my offer. You'll both be sorry if you don't."

"Decisions like this are his to make," Cynthia said. "I wouldn't have it any other way." She stepped with finality through the door Tom held for her.

Turk Loman stood in front of the hotel. The other Bar D men had crossed the street to the store. Over Cynthia's head Tom's gaze met Loman's, and he thought that Loman was sullen for the same reason that Todd was. He had not been on Bar D as long as Todd. Still, he had been a vital part of Dugan's organization, stepping into Todd's shoes just as Todd had stepped into Lew Roman's.

Tom turned toward the livery stable, Cynthia beside him. He was bothered by an uneasy feeling that everything should be settled today, now. He wasn't satisfied with Broncho Quinn's assurance that there would be no trouble Monday. Bonnie might listen to Todd and Loman; she might change her mind.

"Gordon, turn around."

It was Todd's voice. He heard Bonnie's scream, he heard Quinn yell, "No!" He pushed Cynthia off the walk with his left hand and sent her sprawling. He whirled, drawing his revolver as he turned.

Todd and Loman had their guns in their hands. They intended to kill him. There could be no doubt of that. He should have thought of this and driven Todd and Loman out of town before he turned his back to them.

He was slow with his revolver. They were letting him take his time, hoping to convince Quinn that it was a fair fight and not murder. Then, in that last terrible instant, he knew that if he died, the struggle would be lost, that he was as vital to his side as Mike Dugan was to the other.

A gun sounded from out in the street. Loman staggered and spilled forward as Todd squeezed the trigger. Tom felt the bullet tug at the crown of his hat as he fired, his bullet slamming Todd back as if he had been suddenly jerked from behind. His knees gave under him and he fell and rolled over into the dust of the street.

Tom ran toward them as Bert cut across the street. It was Bert who had cut Loman down and so had saved Tom's life. Todd's bullet had been close. He hadn't expected any interference, and the sound of Bert's shot, coming just as Todd was squeezing the trigger, must have thrown him off enough to make him miss his mark.

Doc Sims rushed out of the hotel. Bonnie was still screaming, a high, hysterical sound. Rose put an arm around her and led her back into the hotel. Bert was there then, standing across from Todd's body.

"Thanks," Tom said, and Bert nodded, both staring at Todd.

"I didn't think he'd do it," Bert said. "Not that way."

"I didn't, either," Tom said.

Cynthia was beside him, gripping an arm and shaking it and crying. "I'm all right," he said. "All right. You hear?" She nodded and he said, "I pushed you pretty hard. You aren't hurt?"

"No, of course not." She wiped her eyes. "Is it over? Will there be any more trouble?"

"None we can't handle," Tom said, and again his eyes came to Todd's body and he remembered how he had once thought of him as his friend and how much he owed him, and he turned away as Sims rose from where he had been kneeling beside Loman.

Tom took Cynthia's arm and swung her around. "Let's go home," he said thickly.

He heard Sims say, "Loman's dead."

It didn't seem important. Without Todd, Loman would have been nothing. Tom stumbled and regained his footing, and went on with Cynthia, her anxious eyes on him. She didn't say anything, waiting for him to hook up the mare to the cart when they reached the livery stable.

He gave her a hand, stepped into the seat, and they left town. He noticed that Bert's rifle was still in the street where Arnie had dropped it. He didn't bother with it. Maybe it was a sign of things to come, lying out there in the dust where Arnie had fallen.

He turned upstream, following the road instead of cutting directly across the grass the way they had come. There was no hurry. He looked northwest toward the low hills that hid the Rafter T, and oddly enough, he realized he had never noticed the hills as green as they were now.

He hadn't wanted to kill Todd. He had hoped it would never come to that, but it had, and he could have done nothing except what he did. Todd had tried to kill him, and he had come very close to doing it. Todd had made his choice a long time ago, and Tom, thinking back, knew that what had happened had been inevitable, that it could have ended no other way.

"Funny," he said finally. "I've thought a lot about your dad saying that Dugan's sins would catch up with him, and he'd reap what he sowed. He did, all right, and I hope he lives a long time. The condition he's in is worse than dying."

Cynthia put an arm over his shoulder. She said, "Yes, it will be for him. It might not be for some men, but it will be hell for Mike Dugan." She paused, then added, "A long time ago I wanted you to destroy him. I was wrong. I died a hundred times after you pushed me down. I heard the guns, but I didn't know for a little while whether you were dead or not. All I could think of was that I might have destroyed you, and I couldn't have lived if that had happened. I wouldn't have wanted to."

He looked at her, seeing the love in her eyes, the gentleness, the essential goodness. He said softly, "It's taken a long time to get it through my head how lucky I am. It's foolish to think about the mistakes I've made. I guess we'd better start living for what's ahead."

"Yes," she murmured, "and it's time I quit thinking about the baby I lost. There'll be more who'll live, Tom. I promise you."

"Of course they will," he said. "Of course they will." He didn't have the slightest doubt about it.

Center Point Publishing
600 Brooks Road ● PO Box 1
Thorndike ME 04986-0001 USA

(207) 568-3717

US & Canada:
1 800 929-9108